I0731845

Finding Hope: Faith For The Frustrated

VOLUME 1: RETHINK

Michael S. Rogers

© 2023 by Michael S. Rogers. All rights reserved.

Words Matter Publishing
P.O. Box 1190
Decatur, IL 62525
www.wordsmatterpublishing.com

No part of this publication may be reproduced, stored in a retrieval system, or transmitted in any way by any means—electronic, mechanical, photocopy, recording, or otherwise—without the prior permission of the copyright holder, except as provided by USA copyright law.

ISBN: 978-1-958000-46-5

Library of Congress Catalog Card Number: 2023937785

Dedication

To Irene Coats, Mack Slocum, and Craig Souders,
the first three to shape my own calling
to make disciples.

Table of Contents

PART 3: LIVE

Introduction

I had just turned 32 when the planes hit the towers in New York, and my third child was only months old. I came out of the shower to my wife saying, "You better see this." I watched the towers fall on live television.

We were leaders in our church at the time. I remember how it was those weeks after. Whatever I thought of President Bush over the following years, in the first month, he was the one we needed in leadership at the time. He called on us all to unify and return to our roots. For many, that meant getting back to their roots, their faith.

Our little church in Anderson, Indiana, got ready. Sure enough, people showed up. Vigils, prayer meetings, Sunday morning service attendance—over the next six months, we had every opportunity to speak into peoples' lives. Some of them stayed. Many of them drifted back out of the church. We were satisfied with this one truth: we were given a chance to show people that Jesus is the answer to all their most fundamental questions.

I was 50 when the COVID pandemic hit, and my fourth child was turning twelve. We were moving into a new house on April 1 and had difficulty getting help because everyone was terrified they would get sick. By that time, I was a pastor of fifteen years and led a mid-sized church in Burlington, Indiana. As we had in 2001, our church got ready, but for something completely different.

Churches closed. People isolated. Even small groups shut down. Unlike the last national disaster, people were scattered away from the church. We all faced it in front of television and computer screens, and leaders tried to figure out how to stay relevant as a faith during lockdowns. When the dust cleared, some people came back to church. Many of them drifted out of the church altogether.

I never worked harder as a pastor than I did during the summer of 2020. We would make Plan A in the morning, change to Plan B before the afternoon, and scramble for Plan C before the workday was done. We began to make three plans right from the start, and my job was to call the play and then call audibles when they were necessary. We worked so hard, only for the church to take so many steps backward in its cultural influence.

I'm not blaming anyone, and I'm not going to bash any churches for closing or opening too soon. The point here is not to discuss what the church should have done. Instead, let's talk about reality.

The influence of the church was already changing before the pandemic. All COVID did was give the culture permission to relegate the church to the back of their minds. They were already leaning toward separating the sacred from the secular; the lockdowns helped them see that "real life" could go on without "church."

I'm frustrated by that.

Now, as a leader in the church, I've got a choice to make. I can blame them and talk bad about them and reminisce about "the good old days" when people turned to the church during a disaster (I've actually heard pastors do this!). I can talk about the change in Western culture and how we are post-Christian, and we should just get used to it. I can go "digital" with my ministry and give up trying to get people to make their faith important enough to gather. I can go "phygital" as well, a new term that makes compromises with the culture and offers both a physical and a digital version of "church."

Or I can change ME, personally, before I know what to do about the larger issue.

That's what this series is about—changing me. I thought you might be frustrated, too, so if you're willing to read this, it's also about changing you. I still believe Jesus is the hope of the world and that He called the Church to be His hands and feet and heart and mind to reach the person in front of us. So, I'm calling this series *Finding Hope* because, in the midst of my frustration, God gave me hope for the Church and the culture.

If the change begins with me, then the first volume should deal with *Rethinking My Part*. As the musician Bono once sang in the U2 song *Rejoice*, "I can't change the world, but I can change the world in me, and I rejoice!"

80's alternative children got it. I apologize to the rest of you.

Matthew chapters 5-7 is the recording of the Sermon on the Mount. Though some people consider this a collection of sayings, I see it as the one full-length sermon of Jesus that we have available to us. Since He was the greatest preacher of all time, I asked myself if I could see a pattern.

Jesus said, "KNOW this (Matt 5:1-20), so you can BE this (Matt 5:21-48), and you will LIVE this way (Matt 6:1-7:14), then gave his conclusions at the end (Matt 7:15-27). Know, Be, Live. I decided to fashion my teaching and preaching and now writings in the same way.

Know. First, we must recognize the Tension we are addressing. I learned this from Andy Stanley. Jesus addresses it with the Beatitudes. What tension are we trying to solve? Once we recognize it, what Teaching helps us understand it? Jesus tells us righteousness solves our desire to be blessed.

Be. Then we need to know what we Believe based on the teaching. Jesus asks us to believe our righteousness can be greater than what the Law gave to the Pharisees. If we believe that, then who should we Become? In the Sermon on the Mount, we are asked to become the kind of people who are righteous from our hearts to our obedience instead of from our obedience to our hearts.

Live. If that's true, then how do we live it out? We will give differently, pray differently, and fast differently. If God wants us to love Him with all our heart, soul, mind, and strength, then we should be able to live from those sources. Store up treasures in heaven. Stop being anxious about everything. Set aside the right to judge. Ask, seek, and knock so that we can receive God's gifts, the blessings we crave. Treat others the way we want to be treated.

I believe when Jesus quotes the Great Commandment to love God with *all* our hearts, souls, mind, and strength, that He is giving us a blueprint for change. First, we can't love God with all of anything that is sick or broken. We need His healing in our hearts, souls, mind, and strength first. With that, however, we can rethink how we speak, act, decide, react, and live by walking through those four areas of our lives.

Our hearts are where our treasure is—will it be tuned to the Kingdom of Heaven or the kingdom of me?

Our souls are in dire need of salvation—will we accept that our decision-making is rooted in sinful selfishness and seek help from Jesus?

Our minds naturally conform to this world—will we be transformed as God renews us?

Our strength—our resources, from bodies to finances to societal position—is not enough—will we call on the resurrection power of the Holy Spirit?

None of this is easy; in fact, it's like choosing a narrow gate instead of the wide double doors leading the other way. We are going to challenge those who are Not Yet believers and those who are Already believers in different ways. Let me start here.

Frustrated "Not Yets," we are going to find out what this Christian thing is really all about. I'm asking you to forget everything you've heard about Jesus to this point and honor me as you read by considering Jesus with an open heart and a neutral mind and read at least the first two volumes. If you come into this with a negative mind, why are you even reading this book? If you come in already positive, perhaps you're a ….

Fellow frustrated "Already," we are going to use this format to address our frustrations in this first volume. Then we are going to talk about the Gospel, the Kingdom, the Spirit, the Church, and the Mission. If it worked for Jesus, it can work for us.

So do this for me first.

Pray for an open mind.

Listen for God's heart.

Let peace settle in your soul.

And rise up, Believer. Your King still reigns.

PART 1

KNOW

TENSION: I'm Frustrated, and I Don't Care Who Knows!

I was about to turn twenty-one and had been living on my own for three years. I had already quit a full-ride scholarship for college, had a terrible job I hated, and no direction. My girlfriend's mom, Irene, saw something in me that I didn't see myself. She liked me. I didn't.

"You're so intelligent," she'd say. "Have you thought about this?"

Then she would introduce me to something she had learned from her pastor. I would remark on it in all my worldly wisdom, surprised to find sometimes I agreed with the pastor. I went to church with them a couple of times and was surprised by how friendly they were to the young man in his don't-touch-me clothes. Maybe not all Christians were pompous and self-righteous, after all.

Then she challenged me to listen to a sermon she had on cassette tape (yes, I'm *that* old). Called "The Wonder of His

Healing," the teaching was from this guy Bob Russell from a church in Louisville called Southeast Christian. She had been so kind and complimentary, and my girlfriend (her name was Faith) was going to be a while before she got home from work, so I went into their living room and popped in the tape.

Pastor Russell talked about a guy who had been disabled all his life. He claimed he didn't want to be but had fallen to a last resort. He heard this rumor about angels making bubbles in a pool that would heal anything. So, he went to it, sat by it, and waited.

Must've been some kind of hot spring because occasionally, the water would boil just like they said. But he could never get into the pool first. Someone always beat him, and he had lost all hope. Then Jesus comes by and sees him lying there, knowing he had been there a long time. He walks up to the man, maybe puts a hand on his shoulder, and looks him in the eye.

"Do you want to be healed?"

Pastor Russell said this was a loaded question because getting healed was going to create change. He would have to take care of himself. He would have to maybe find a job, go back to help take care of his parents, and maybe become a part of the community again. He would have to tell his story over and over again. Everything would change. I hadn't thought of it that way.

Then Pastor Russell dropped the bomb on me. I'm paraphrasing from my memory here, but he basically said we would have to start one step earlier. At least this man knew he was sick. We were sick, and we didn't even know it. To answer the question, "Do you want to be healed?" we had to first answer the question, "Do you know you are sick?"

Jesus met me right there. Tenderly, He showed me I *was* sick. Sick and tired. Lost. Alone among my family and friends. Directionless. Worse, I was selfish, mean sometimes, used and abused the people around me. I knew I didn't like myself. I didn't know it was because I was sick, and I hated it.

In my mind's eye, that heartsick twenty-year-old, tears in his eyes, said out loud, "Yes."

I'm sick, and I want to be healed. I accepted Jesus right there and was baptized four months later after learning everything I could about what it meant to be healed. Well, everything I *thought* I could learn.

Why do I bring up this story? Because I admit, I am *still* learning how sick I am and that I need healing. Don't worry, I'm not questioning my salvation. I'm just admitting that God is still not allowed in some of the places I don't want Him to see. As if He needed my permission!

I guard those areas closely because they feel right for me. Maybe not always, but often enough that I still want to indulge in that selfishness. No plan here to delve into my deep dark underbelly. I'm just leading you to a truth that we might share. In many of those areas that still need healing, I tell myself I am experiencing righteous indignation—a legitimate term and a real possibility that I often use to cover my proud assessment of the things that need fixing.

In other words, the things that frustrate me.

That's the tension we must address first. What are we so frustrated about, and why?

I've made a list of those frustrations over the next few pages. Yes! I have this many frustrations! Maybe you can relate to one or two of them. As you read, I'd like you to consider three things.

1. Notice these frustrations are legitimate.
2. Watch how often they are over circumstances too large for me to fix on my own.
3. Listen for the truly righteous heartache they bring, almost like realizing there is a disability that I can't seem to fix, and how they relate to the man by the Pool of Bethesda in John 5:1-17.

I'M FRUSTRATED WITH MY FAITH

Here I am, a pastor of sixteen years and a Christian now for thirty, and I am *still* going back and back and back to the rudiments of the faith. I'm still struggling with my sin, still struggling with hearing His still small voice, still unable to understand and explain the basics of the Gospel to lost people. Worse, and I hope I'm the only one but fear it is too common, I still struggle sometimes with the validity of what I believe.

How is this possible? I've been teaching and preaching and counseling long enough to be considered an expert. I have two degrees and a long list of successes. I have battle scars from failures that turned out to be blessings. I can list a litany of answered prayers that were this side of miraculous, some that without a doubt deserve that adjective. How can I still be such a babe in my faith?

Hasn't God done enough to show me He is real?

The answer is yes. Today. Right this minute. Yes, He has blessed me beyond measure. He has broken the cycle of generational curses and environment in my life. The listless kid of twenty is now a husband blessed with a great wife, the father of four great kids, and the called one of God to help lead the charge of God's Kingdom for the sake of the prisoners in darkness. Spiritually, mentally, socially, and financially, He has freed me from so much that I can't help but praise Him. Every time Brandon Lake's song *Gratitude* plays, I become a blubbering idiot of praise.

And yet.

- Too often, I ignore Him to do my own selfish thing.
- Too often, I listen for Him and then debate whether He's the one talking to me or not.
- Too often, I get an opportunity to share the Gospel and realize I'm unsure how to start or finish.
- Too often, I hear something that seems to oppose the Word of God and I question the Word instead of waiting to understand.
- Too often, I get angry about something the church is or isn't doing and rail at her.

That frustrates me. Shouldn't I be better equipped by now? Because, to be honest . . .

I'M FRUSTRATED WITH MY SALVATION

I already said I was not questioning my salvation. The frustration doesn't come from any doubt about that. Hmm. Isn't that funny? I'm frustrated with my level of faith, but it doesn't affect my belief that I am saved.

See? That's what frustrates me about it!

I know too many people who see their relationship with Jesus as something more like fire insurance than Lordship. When we get baptized, most of us have made a confession that "Jesus is the Christ, the Son of the Living God, that He is my Lord and Savior…."

Why am I so good at trusting Him for salvation but so bad at obeying Him as Lord?

That frustration comes down to a feeling that I've been treated to the old bait and switch. You know what I mean? The local car dealership tells everyone they can have 0% interest with payments as low as $200 a month. You get excited and go down there only to find that you don't have the right credit and you need a down payment of $5,000. You can still have the car, though, but at 18% interest and payments of $450 a month.

I was told that grace was a free gift and that I didn't need to earn anything. That God would transform me and that I would only need to believe in Him to have eternal life. But oh, by the way, you need to stop dressing like that, and you can't talk that way, and you can't dance, smoke or chew or go with girls that do.

I got a healthy dose of what I was saved from, but I wasn't told until after my commitment what I was saved to. Now, to be honest, the church where I was baptized was great at trying to share this with me. I have to admit this was the attitude of the members of the church around me more than the teaching of the leaders. Still, I was confused.

If grace is free, why do I need to change?

And if I'm saved, what does it matter?

As a leader in the church, I've tried to understand why so many people would come and have an experience with Jesus, believe in Him, and get baptized, then fall away from church and sometimes even faith afterward. Maybe, I thought, it was too little gratitude. Or maybe we've struggled to give the whole Gospel to those who would believe. Which is why . . .

I'M FRUSTRATED WITH CHURCH MEMBERS

Somehow, we bought the lie that Sunday morning service *is* church. I've approached members who have attended hundreds of sermons, hundreds of Bible studies, and hundreds of small groups, who will tell me they don't know enough to share the Gospel with their friends. How can that be true? Worse, that isn't the real issue. My fear and frustration are that they'd rather bring the person to church than be uncomfortable try-ing to share the Good News.

That might be harsh. I fear it's not harsh enough. Some of those people haven't invited anyone to church in a long time.

I met a young man who came to one of our interest meet-ings for our church plant. He asked great questions and wanted to know what the purpose of our new expression of faith would be. That interview was exciting to me because I believed I had met someone who understood we couldn't continue to do church as a social club.

Then I went to lunch with him and found out he was an atheist. He attended church for the social aspect alone. That I really believed Jesus could change the world intrigued him. Somehow, he had missed that part of church in the years he had been attending.

My fear is that we are no longer engaged in the mission of Christ but are engaged in a mission to have people join our particular church culture. We don't share the Gospel out of fear that we are in over our heads. We invite people to church, though, because it's easier to assimilate them into our culture. Believe like us. Be like us. Act like us. Talk like us.

That's why we have jokes about certain denominations having their own space in heaven because they don't know other Christians are there.

Many people know how St. Patrick brought Christianity to Ireland. But do they know about Palladius? He was the first missionary to Ireland, sent by Pope Celestine I. He failed partly because he believed in converting the Irish to Christianity, but he first had to Romanize them. How could they understand what Christ had done for them if they weren't civilized?

St. Patrick, on the other hand, was called to the Irish by God and saw them for who they were. He knew they believed in the supernatural and in the power of the number three. Using the shamrock, he explained the Trinity and the God who died for them and unleashed the Holy Spirit for all mankind. In other words, he saw how God could speak to the Irish from their culture and used that to bring salvation to the island. (*Celtic Evangelism* by George Hunter III is a great resource for this story.)

This is so much more difficult, but it is also more effective. Our members must rethink what it means to be the Church and learn that the church culture they create is not as important as reaching the lost for the King of Heaven. We can't just be a collective brought together by our beliefs; we are a community of believers brought together to fulfill the mission. They won't make it easy on us, which is why…

I'M FRUSTRATED WITH THE ORGANIZED CHURCH

I mean the "Big C" Church. Not any one church or any one denomination or any one particular worship style. For many years, I have been a fan of the diversity in the Church and celebrated the fact that most denominations can be praised for getting something right and convicted of getting something wrong. That's why, when people ask me, I tell them I'm

MethoBaptiNazaPenteChristiVineyOlic. I'm the *Heinz 57* mutt for Jesus.

But I'm frustrated by all of them. Some are just off their rockers when it comes to the Word. They've decided that the Word can be reinterpreted based on the culture of the day. Can't truck with that, don't want to deal with them right now. Don't need to point it out; so many others are doing it for me.

I'm talking about the ones who are staying true to the Word but are not helping to accomplish the mission. Once, I went to get my haircut, and my stylist found out I was a pastor. He asked if I ever teach the End Times (I could hear the capital letters when he said the words). I told him I don't shy away from preaching on the end times but that they are not my focus.

He almost lost his mind. Wasn't that the mission of the church, to warn the people that the end times were coming? To identify and thwart the Anti-Christ? To be aware of the schemes of the devil? He was so sure that he was right he wouldn't let me answer his question. Of course, he also proved through some pretty fancy wordplay that Donald Trump was the Anti-Christ. Some of you might agree with him, but don't get sidetracked.

Here's my point. Guy like that, we can shake our heads and listen to his conspiracy theories and wonder how anyone could get so hung up on one part of Christianity that they've forgotten the central mission. But many of our churches are the same. We substitute Donald Trump as the Anti-Christ with

Republicans or Democrats and say our job is to win elections. We put more thought into the comfort of the saved than the condition of the lost. We want to clean up our city streets instead of sharing our witness.

Don't get me wrong. I think Christians should be involved in politics and social justice, and I think God directly tells us to take care of the household of God first. But those aren't the *mission*. And while we forfeit the mission, everything around us is falling apart. Which is why…

I'M FRUSTRATED WITH THE WORLD

Hey, I'm old enough to use the phrase, "Kids these days…." But I don't. Know why? Because I raised kids that aren't acting like most kids these days. They have their flaws, sure, but they are walking reminders to me that the real issue is us. We *should* be saying, "Parents these days…."

If I believe in God, then in His Word, He tells me there is an enemy in the spiritual realm. He is called the prince of this world, and he is real. He doesn't wear a red suit or own a pitchfork. Instead, he owns deception and confusion, and he prowls around to see who is primed to be devoured.

His fingerprints are all over the world we live in today. We are confused about love, about life, about truth. Our leaders, regardless of affiliation, lie so often that we don't really know who to trust anymore. The school system thinks the parents should be banned from their kids, and the parents think the school system should be avoided. The solution offered for racial tension is more racial tension. We have new terms like "fake news" and "disinformation," and we are more divided than we've ever been.

And that's just America.

Around the world, so many dreadful things are happening. It frustrates me because most of the people I meet are decent. If most of us are decent, how can we be so, well, demonic as a whole? That frustrates me. The only thing I know to do is share the Gospel with the next person in front of me, which is why…

I'M FRUSTRATED WITH EVANGELISM

This tags onto my frustration with church members, but it's deeper. Some time ago, a teacher in the church thought teaching discipleship would be easier if he could break it down into two levels—one for the Already Believing and one for those Not Yet Believers. Brilliant idea for his time.

Problems began, though, when the church played its version of the telephone game and lost the original message. We started believing discipleship was for believers and evangelism was for seekers, and that they were divorced from each other. In a way, they are. When we separate them, though, we run the risk of overemphasizing one or the other and missing the connection between the two.

If we don't disciple people to evangelize, the church starts believing only the pastor and a select few do it. If we don't evangelize to disciple, the church starts filling with people who believe they are saved but don't know what to do next. If we pair the two into disciple-making, we will have mature disciples so that they become disciple-makers.

This won't be easy, partly because we've lived with the separation for so long. Just remember the initial separation happened because someone was struggling to mature people into disciple-makers, which means the issue has been around longer than the separation. That frustrates me! Which is why...

I'M FRUSTRATED TRYING TO UNDERSTAND THE HOLY SPIRIT

Not to make too fine a point, but it may be this last frustration is the precursor to all the others. Because I don't completely understand the Holy Spirit, I get the feeling now that I'm saved and trying to be faithful that everything I do to help relieve my frustrations is in my own power.

Therein lies madness. Earlier, I quoted Bono from U2 when he wrote, "I can't change the world, but I can change the world in me, and I rejoice."

But that isn't true, is it? I can't change myself, either. I can only rejoice when I understand the power of the Spirit to change me and, through that, influence the world. I don't just want to understand the third person of the Trinity; I want to share what I learn with other frustrated believers.

WRAPPING IT UP

Did you do what I asked? Did you consider the three questions? Let me remind you what they were:

1. Notice that the frustrations are legitimate.
2. Watch how often they are over circumstances too large for me to fix on my own.
3. Listen for the truly righteous heartache they bring, almost like realizing there is a disability that I can't seem to fix, and how they relate to the man by the Pool of Bethesda in John 5:1-17.

I'm embarrassed to point out the obvious here, but it's why I'm committed to writing this series. All seven of my frustrations are legitimate, and all seven are too large for me to fix on my own. Only one makes me answer the question.

Do I really want to be healed?

I can't change the world by myself. I can't change the Church by myself. I can't change how the Gospel is preached by myself. I can't even change myself by myself.

But I can admit I am sick and let the Healer do His thing, so that's where this first volume starts.

I just have to rethink my part.

TEACHING: Frustration Can't Be My Motivation

I guess it's possible you went through the Tension and couldn't identify with me on any of it. Praise God! Many of us are lost in that frustration, though, so if you aren't, please keep reading. Hopefully, this will give you tools to help the ones around you who seem to be largely motivated by one of those frustrations.

Some of you may have taken offense. I realize what I have done. I have shared my perspective on our situation, and you may rightly accuse me of being anecdotal. You don't have one or more of these frustrations because your experience is different than mine. Again, praise God! Many of us are in that situation, though, so if you aren't, keep reading. My fellow frustrated may be in the church right down the street from you or sitting at home because they can't find what you have. Share it!

If you are one of the frustrated, I've got great news for you! Your frustration is not sinful. Being motivated by your frustration, though, can lead you into some bad habits. Don't believe me?

Look at Judas and Jesus.

JUDAS WAS CALLED

First, let's consider how we know Judas at all. We catch up with Jesus in the sixth chapter of Luke, right after he has announced, "The Son of Man is Lord of the Sabbath." He's healed on that day of rest, and the authorities are furious with him. They are already trying to decide what to do with Jesus.

In these days, He [Jesus] went out to the mountain to pray, and all night He continued in prayer to God. And when day came, He called His disciples and chose from them twelve, whom He named apostles…

— Luke 6:12-13

As was His regular habit, Jesus approached a major decision by spending extended time in conversation with His Father. He didn't make the choices He would announce lightly. He wanted to be sure those choices were informed and blessed.

That means Judas was expected by God to be part of that group (Luke 6:16). He was in the ministry with Jesus for years. He experienced what the others experienced: healings, casting out of demons, and challenges to the status quo. Everything they experienced, he experienced.

Lazy theologians will say that Judas was chosen *because* he would betray Christ. I'm not saying they are wrong—God knew, and Jesus knew (John 6:70 & 13:27)—just that they are incomplete. We can't believe God gives us free will and believe Judas couldn't make any other choice.

So—what led him to betray Jesus?

JUDAS WAS FRUSTRATED

In my study, I've come to believe the root of his actions is frustration.

Jesus has just described His mystical qualities at the beginning of the sixth chapter of John. He compares Himself to the manna from Heaven given to the Israelites during the Exodus. He said some pretty disturbing things about eating His body and drinking His blood and that eternal life is found in Him, and that while He was teaching in the synagogue!

The Jews of that day were looking for something different. Many of the disciples were confused or offended. Jesus knew among those who were most confused was Judas. John hints at it at the end of the chapter.

Jesus said to the Twelve, "Do you want to go away as well?" Simon Peter answered Him, "Lord, to whom shall we go? You have the words of eternal life, and we have believed, and have come to know that you are the Holy

One of God. Jesus answered them, "Did I not choose you, the Twelve? And yet one of you is a devil."

— John 6:67-70

Jesus hints to us that He could see the frustration in Judas. All this talk of bodies and blood and eternal life. What about the Roman occupation? What about liberating Israel? Many disciples walked away during that time, and Jesus called out the apostles. Though Peter answers for all of them, something in Judas causes Jesus to tip off the ending. John realizes later what Jesus was doing and finishes the chapter with:

He spoke of Judas, the son of Simon Iscariot, for he, one of the Twelve, was going to betray him.

— John 6:71

FURTHER EVIDENCE

Is it surprising, then, that the apostle's frustration becomes more evident when Mary anoints Jesus' feet with expensive perfume and her hair? John is quick to point out that Judas is a thief and that he saw himself losing money. Such a rich gift "wasted" on the feet of Jesus (John 12:6)! Is that any less frustrating?

But Judas Iscariot, one of his disciples (he who was about to betray him), said, "Why was this ointment not sold for three hundred denarii and given to the poor?"

— John 12:5

I have a confession to make. I grumble when I drive. Why? Because of all the people around me who don't know how to drive. Of course, that's my personal opinion. That doesn't make me wrong.

Behind the wheel is where I am most vulnerable to frustration. I want to get somewhere, and all these people are in the way! You might think after reading this that I am often the victim of road rage, but that isn't true. Road rage would be way too obvious a sin. I'd much rather grumble under my breath about the intelligence of my road companions (or lack thereof).

My kids will read this and laugh. Grumble? More like shout!

It always seemed less…well, sinful. Until my kids got old enough to learn how to drive, and I saw in them what I had taught by osmosis. I'm still trying to fix that sin, but it's relevant here because my frustration is sometimes warranted and sometimes self-induced. Maybe the other driver shouldn't have made that decision, but the real issue is that I can't get to where I want to go or can't get there as fast as I would like.

My frustration isn't a sin, but my response to it is.

I think Judas is suffering from the same thing in this passage. As I read the quote, I couldn't help hearing a deeper frustration than the money he lost. The Christ was supposed to be a king and a liberator, but He had spent all His time among the poor, the downtrodden, the sick, the demon-possessed. The heat is increasing around them after Jesus raises Lazarus from the dead. The Pharisees and scribes are looking for a way to get rid of this teacher who seems to have unexplained supernatural power.

The time is ripe for the King of Israel to make Himself known, and all He has done is serve the least of these. Then Mary comes along and wastes a year's salary on Jesus' feet. Shouldn't He be outraged? He talks about being a physician for the sick and serving the least, but He's okay with this.

Sure, Judas is going to lose money on this. But also, isn't Jesus betraying even what Judas would call this lesser vision of who the Messiah is? How can He do that and still be who He says He is? And then, Jesus responds by saying we'll always have the poor but will not always have Him. From Judas' perspective, wouldn't this sound like hubris?

Maybe I should pause here and reassure the reader. I am not excusing Judas. I am trying to live in his shoes for a few paragraphs to emphasize my point. Judas didn't understand what Jesus was doing, didn't understand who Jesus was, and he got frustrated. So, what did he do about it? In Matthew's version, this story is followed by an account of the life of Judas.

Then one of the Twelve, whose name was Judas Iscariot, went to the chief priests and said, "What will you give me if I deliver him over to you?" And they paid him thirty pieces of silver. And from that moment, he sought an opportunity to betray him.

— Matthew 26:14-16

A recognition of the frustration of Judas doesn't give him an out for what he did, and it doesn't make light of what John says about Satan entering Judas at the Last Supper (John 13:27). It does shed some light on how the enemy worked on him to get him to do what he did despite all he had seen accomplished by Jesus and the apostles. Despite what he likely had accomplished himself.

Remember, Judas was with the Twelve when Jesus said he saw Satan fall like lightning because of what they had accomplished on the mission field (Luke 10:18). Frustration motivated him to forget all he had learned about Jesus and ended in betrayal, death, suicide, and shame.

JESUS GOT FRUSTRATED, TOO

My wife and I like to look at the passages where we find "Salty Jesus." We call it that when he seems to live on the edge of throwing His hands in the air and forgetting the whole thing. Like right after he feeds the 4,000, and the group crosses the lake to Dalmanutha. The Pharisees meet Him there right after all these miracles and asks Him for a sign from heaven.

> *And he [Jesus} sighed deeply in his spirit and said, "Why does this generation seek a sign? Truly, I say to you, no sign will be given to this generation." And he left them, got into the boat again, and went to the other side.*
>
> *— Mark 8:11-13*

Do you feel the frustration in the sigh that is "deep in His spirit" and in how quickly He gets back in the boat? Jesus is frustrated here, but He doesn't lash out or plan the demise of the Pharisees. Instead, He responds by letting them know no sign will be enough, and then He walks away.

The most famous incident for Salty Jesus is when he clears out the temple. We read about Him driving out the moneychangers and not letting anyone come into the temple. Can you imagine? Jesus comes at them with force and responds not only to what the moneychangers are doing but what the general population is doing by using them. Yes, the moneychangers are at fault; but they are only the most obvious symptom of the deeper illness.

The leaders and the people are using them for their worship and sacrifice. So, Jesus not only turns over the tables, He won't let anyone complete their shameful practices at all. That's pretty frustrating. How can we reconcile this response with the last? Read earlier in the chapter for context.

And he entered Jerusalem and went into the temple. And when he had looked around at everything, as it was already late, he went out to Bethany with the Twelve.
— Mark 11:11

Before His tirade, he saw the situation, no doubt felt the frustration immediately and went to a safe place to consider what to do. Nowhere in this passage does it tell us Jesus prayed, but that was so much a part of His way of doing things; can we doubt it? A night away and a return to the scene with prayer in between allowed Him to know the right way to respond.

Turns out, His initial reaction was backed up by God's approval. Harsh, yes, but He made His point and He did it under the authority of his Father.

One last instance of frustration occurs in the Garden of Gethsemane. Here, Jesus is pouring out His heart on the last night of freedom, asking God to let His cup of wrath pass from him. He even pleads with God to find another way. The prayer is so intense that blood and sweat mingle from his pores. He is beyond himself in anguish.

All He asked his apostles, His closest friends, to do was be there for him and pray for Him. And they fell asleep. Not once, not twice, but three times. Whatever excuses we can make for them, imagine the frustration in Jesus. He spent three years teaching them, loving them, living with them, and has been there for everyone else's needs during that time. Now He prepares to spend His blood for them, and they can't even stay awake?

Yet Jesus responds with grace and truth anyway. Truth by calling them out for it, grace by loving them anyway, and going through with the sacrifice.

FOLLOW JUDAS OR FOLLOW JESUS

One of the ways Jesus ups the ante on our obedience in the Sermon on the Mount is that He takes several of the Ten Commandments and says, "Not only is it wrong to do this, but it's wrong to think of doing it!" The Jews knew adultery and murder were wrong. But they allowed the intent to fill their hearts by lusting and hating.

Jesus doesn't just want us to obey the Letter of the Law. He wants us to obey the Spirit. We can see this most clearly in Paul's writing.

> *But now we are released from the law, having died to that which held us captive, so that we serve in the new way of the Spirit and not in the old way of the written code.*
>
> *— Romans 7:6*

Paul isn't proposing in this chapter that we no longer be obedient to God's commandments. He's setting us up to tell us we will be *even more* righteous if we walk in the Spirit. We'll develop this concept in a later volume, but for now, this is my point:

When we get frustrated, *it doesn't matter if we are right!*

Let me say that again without yelling. When we get frustrated, it doesn't matter if we are right. This was an important lesson for me because I always felt that if I was right—and especially if I was right and on God's side—I had the authority through "righteous indignation" to act however I wanted.

JUDAS BELIEVED HE WAS RIGHT

He wasn't, but he thought he was. This couldn't be the Messiah because He didn't fit what Judas was expecting. Judas got frustrated and eventually thought this man had to be stopped. If He wasn't the Messiah, He was a deceiver. After Mary's perfume bath, Judas convinced himself He wasn't the Messiah He made Himself out to be, so he reacted immediately.

Believing he was justified, Judas went to the authorities to betray Jesus. We are near the end here but notice that Judas lives in that misunderstanding right up until the kiss in the garden. Why is that important to see? Because of all Jesus did between the decision and the kiss, that proved He was the Messiah. Miracles, teaching, prayers, service. Look especially at this passage from John:

(Hold on. Before I include this quote, I want us to admit something to each other. I've read the Bible through several times, and I've read Christian books often. My tendency is to skip the large quoted sections or to skim through them to get the main idea. I look at the reference and think, "Yeah, I know where that is." Don't do that this time. Read this passage with new eyes and remember *Judas is still in the room):*

During supper, when the devil had already put it into the heart of Judas Iscariot, Simon's son, to betray Him, Jesus, knowing that the Father had given all things into His hands and that He had come from God and was going back to God, rose from supper. He laid aside His outer garments and, taking a towel, tied it around His waist. Then He poured water into a basin and began to wash the disciples' feet and to wipe them with the towel that was wrapped around Him.

— John 13:2-5

Catch that? Satan had already convinced Judas. Jesus still washed his feet. And yet, Judas allowed the enemy to trap him in the misunderstanding.

Later, his remorse is going to get the better of him. Right at the moment, while he feels he is right, he reacts immediately and then lives unwilling to admit he might be wrong. This permits him to take the final, fateful step and hold unswervingly to it.

He crafted his own response to his frustration. "I know what I'll do. The Pharisees have been looking for a way, asking after someone willing to put an end to this man. I'll show him." He may even have thought that if Jesus was really the Messiah, He would have to show Himself when the Pharisees came to kill Him.

All this imagining about Judas' mindset is speculation, of course, but stay with me. Even if what I've constructed about his thought process is wrong, my assessment of his response to frustration still holds:

- He reacted immediately.
- He lived in that misunderstanding and refused to consider new evidence to the contrary.
- He crafted his own response.

JESUS IS DIFFERENT

In the three examples I gave, we see Jesus responding differently. Instead of letting His frustration provoke Him to an immediate reaction, He walked away from what frustrated Him. Although He felt right about His assessment, He gave Himself time to pray before deciding what to do. When He did respond, His Father helped Him craft the response with grace and truth.

Disciples during this time didn't just learn lessons in lectures and small group discussions. They lived with their Rabbi and saw how he handled himself in every situation. Discovering his character and his will, they chose to mimic him as much as they could. We would be wise to do the same as we learn to follow Jesus. When we feel frustrated, we can follow this three-step process.

- Walk away
- Pray
- Respond under the authority of God with grace and truth.

PART 2

BE: A RETHINKER

BELIEVE: I Need To Rethink My Response

I believe Jesus lives in the "Be" of His lessons. When we get a grip on what He means by telling us we can't just avoid adultery but must think differently, we are asked to be the kind of person who doesn't see other humans as sexual objects for our delight. He doesn't deny the pleasure of sex—God made it to be fun!—but He is telling us we too often see sex from a selfish point of view.

To be different from the world, we become the kind of people who think differently. Jesus gives us some great examples of how we should think differently in the Sermon on the Mount. These lessons could cure most of the evil that is happening in the world today.

Don't just avoid murder; avoid hating others.

Don't just avoid adultery; avoid sexualizing others.

Don't just marry; be faithful.

Don't just make promises; keep them.

Don't just exact equal vengeance; forgive.

Don't just love your neighbors; love your enemies.

Think of how different the world would be today if we were all loving, selfless, full of integrity, honest, dependable, and forgiving. Jesus says, "Don't just act differently, *be* different."

But to be different, we must think differently.

The word *repent* is thrown around a lot in Christian circles. I sometimes wonder if we realize how powerful it really is. When I've had the opportunity to teach and preach on it, I've often focused on the closeness of God when we decide to turn back to Him.

In one sermon, I had an associate come onto the platform to help me demonstrate. I faced him and told the congregation that this was what it was like to be close to God. Facing Him, vulnerable, able to see Him, and admitting I am being seen.

But when I do something He won't approve, it's like I turn my back on Him. Each thing I do that goes against Him feels like one more step away from Him. My associate would remain stationary as I listed sins I might commit and took steps away. By the end of it, I was on the other side of the platform, far away from God.

"To turn back to Him, then," I said, "would mean a long trek back to the intimacy I enjoyed at the beginning." Turning around, I would note the distance between God and me. "But that's not what repentance is like."

I would return to face God, re-establish that intimate connection, and repeat how I had turned away from God and was taking steps away from Him. Only this time, my associate would follow me across the platform so that when I turned around, He was there to embrace me.

Proud of that one, really. It demonstrates how God is not waiting with a tapping toe for us to realize the error of our ways and then make us come crawling back to Him after we repent. All this is true. To repent means, in a way, to turn back.

But it is so much more than this re-establishment of my connection with God. Here's where we get confused in the church. This view of repentance is all about me. My position, my sin, my admission, my redemption.

Repentance, however, is more about God than about us. If we are learning about the character of God and find ourselves in the starring role, we are missing something. That doesn't mean I have to scrap what I've learned. Repentance does mean to turn back to God, and our Father is waiting to embrace us as soon as we turn. But it is so much more. Repentance isn't just saying I'm sorry and being confident I will be forgiven.

TO REPENT IS TO RETHINK

Peter replied, "Repent and be baptized, every one of you, in the name of Jesus Christ for the forgiveness of your sins. And you will receive the gift of the Holy Spirit.
— Acts 2:38

This passage directly follows Peter's first sermon, where he tells the Jews during Pentecost that they killed their Messiah, but

He rose again to save them. As Jews, they have been taught that animal sacrifice atones for their sin. They are now learning someone loved them enough to die for them and powerful enough to beat the grave and conquer death for them. But they aren't surprised to find they are sinful and need to turn back to God.

Peter isn't just saying, "Admit you weren't righteous enough and then get wet." He is calling them to *rethink* what they have believed about God in the name of Jesus. Strong's Concordance says the Greek word translated as repent is *metanoeo* and defines it as, "I repent, change my mind, change the inner man…."

Peter is saying, "You were wrong when you refused to believe that Jesus is the Christ. Rethink your position and commit to the one who can truly save you from your sin." We'll deal with the Spirit in a later volume, but here let's note that the Spirit is our reward for rethinking and committing to Jesus. My favorite verse that addresses this doesn't use the word repentance. But see it with new eyes:

> *Do not be conformed to this world, but be transformed by the renewal of your mind, that by testing, you may discern what is the will of God, what is good and acceptable and perfect.*
>
> *— Romans 12:2*

This is true repentance. We stop conforming to the world's way of thinking and let the Spirit transform our thinking so that we can discern what God wants for us and from us. Remember the frustrations I listed for us in the Tension?

1. My faith
2. My salvation
3. Church members
4. The Church
5. The world
6. Evangelism
7. Understanding the Spirit

I asked the reader to notice three things about these frustrations. Here's a reminder of those:

1. Notice that the frustrations are legitimate.
2. Watch how often they are over circumstances too large for me to fix on my own.
3. Listen for the truly righteous heartache they bring, almost like realizing there is a disability that I can't seem to fix, and how they relate to the man by the Pool of Bethesda in John 5:1-17.

Every frustration comes from issues I consider legitimate. Often, my reaction is immediate when I am faced with them. I grumble just like I do when I'm driving. Sometimes I scream and shout. I can be extremely opinionated and cruelly assumptive in these moments.

My frustration becomes motivation to lash out. Even when I want something to change, I sometimes neglect the steps to take in the right direction so that I can continue to lash out. I've crafted my responses so well that I literally fall into the same sentences to describe my frustration when I'm telling someone new about them.

This is how Judas would respond.

Although I find I am frustrated with myself sometimes, most often I'm frustrated with something else so big it is beyond my control. I don't have the power to fix it, but I believe I can see it better than anyone else. I mull over all the terrible things happening in the Church, with Church people, and in the world, and I can't stand it!

I also can't change it. So, I live in the misunderstanding, craft my witty retorts, and satisfy myself with iron defenses for my position.

This is how Judas would respond.

The frustrations often leave me heartsick. I don't want to doubt my God, feel like His salvation for me is a bait and switch. It deeply moves me that the Church is not all she was intended to be. Division, pettiness, judgment, pride. I want my children to grow up in a world based on righteousness, not confusion and deception, anxiety and dismay.

So, I look for the worst of it. I do. Sometimes, when the wrong party is in power and the economy is struggling, and I'm watching the news as the Dow Jones loses points, I'm almost gleeful when it drops more because it proves my position. At that moment, I don't care about the money lost by retirees and investors. I just want to be right.

This is how Judas would respond.

I NEED TO RETHINK EVERYTHING

God is big enough to change everything that frustrates me. He can change the world through the power of His Gospel. He can disciple church members into disciple-makers instead of consumers and spectators. He can revive the Bride of Christ and remind her of the mission. How does He do that? He tells us in His Word. How can I help Him?

By believing the first person who needs to change is me.

BECOME: Humble Enough To Change

I promised myself I would be brutally honest if I got the chance to write all this down, so here goes. It ticks me off that God makes me start here. Gets my dander up. Causes me to flush with anger.

Why? Where does this emotion originate? In my pride, of course.

I'm the one that sees the problems! I'm the one that has come up with solutions! I'm the one that cares enough to call it out! Why do I have to be the first one to change?

Pride.

Doubting my faith or getting confused about my salvation doesn't make me different from anyone else. Anger at the church? Get in line. Worried about the direction of the world? No monopoly on that feeling. My frustration may arrive differently, and I may express it differently, but the wise King Solomon tells me nothing is new under the sun.

Everything that frustrates me has one thing in common: my perspective. I am seeing the world from my point of view and deciding how it should be fixed according to my will. Sometimes my will is the same as God's will. I'm really proud of that.

My pride is not new, but it is unique to me. Because it is not new, I can find the remedy in God's Word. Because it is unique to me, how God changes me will be tailored to me.

In one of the Psalms, David starts out with a selfish perspective. He asks God to lift him up, to keep him from being put to shame, and to help him have victory over his enemies. He even calls on God to shame the "wantonly treacherous." He's building up a good rant. If it were me, I'd just go on from there to describe how shameful these people are. In other places, David does that, too! But here, he is stopped by something. A new thought enters his mind just as he revs his motor.

> *Make me to know Your ways, O Lord; teach me Your paths. Lead me in Your truth and teach me, for You are the God of my salvation; for You, I wait all the day long.*
> *— Psalm 25:4-5*

Right when he is about to blast his opponents, he realizes he is getting worked up. Where does he turn? To God's teaching. To His way, not David's. That he continues with a request is telling.

Remember not the sins of my youth or my transgressions; according to Your steadfast love remember me, for the sake of Your goodness, O Lord!

— Psalm 25:7

Just as he is tempted to tell God about the sinfulness of his enemies, David asks God to forgive him for his own sins. When he has done this, he is ready to see the reality of God and the reality of his own role before Him.

Good and upright is the Lord; therefore, He instructs sinners in the way. He leads the humble in what is right and teaches the humble His way. All the paths of the Lord are steadfast love and faithfulness for those who keep His covenant and His testimonies.

— Psalm 25:8-10

Who are the sinners David mentions? All of them! His enemies and himself. Seeing his plight from that perspective, he realizes the focal point, the "star of the show," is not himself or his enemies. God gets that role. All need His instruction in the way to be steadfast in love and faithful to the covenant God has offered.

Despite the real possibility that all my frustrations are legitimate and that my assessment of the condition of the Church and the world might be correct, the real issue God wants me to deal with is me. Here is where He can start to influence both.

His Kingdom doesn't start with me; it starts with Him. But my next responsibility is to bring myself into alignment with Him, not the Church or the world.

If enough of us humble ourselves to realize our immense need for His instruction, we will become His instrument to bring the needed change in the larger scheme of things.

MORE HONESTY

My greatest fear is that I am writing this more to justify the next volumes than to take into my heart what I am saying. I know this is a real danger for me. Wouldn't that be ironic? To write a book promoting humility but, in my pride, use it to rail at the rest of mankind for God's benefit?

I have to really pause here and pray. Am I willing, in real life, to lay down my frustration as motivation and humble myself to wait, to pray, and to act only under the authority of my Father? Will I recognize, like David, my own need to humble myself, and rethink (repent of) the sins I have committed out of frustration and (gasp) in the name of Jesus Christ?

Fellow frustrated, this is where the healing of the Church and the world begin.

I am a sinner in the hands of a merciful God, full of grace and truth, who wishes to reach every human being with the Good News of Jesus Christ. I have heard and believed that Good News and repented of (rethought) my way of life, found myself wanting, and put my faith in the power of His death, burial, and resurrection to save me. He is still remaking me as I give allegiance to Him and His covenants and commandments and testimonies. He is the center of the universe, not me.

I recognize His position, His supremacy. I recognize my position, my subordination. Because I trust Him, I submit to His authority and relinquish my right to be right. No matter how frustrated I get, He gets to determine my response.

Humble me first, Father, that I may in humility speak to my brother and my sister about Your greatness.

THE NEXT STEP

Maybe there isn't one, really. A next step. Maybe this step is all the steps wrapped in one.

I'm sitting here as I type the first draft, wondering if I really understand what I'm teaching (and if I'll have the courage to keep this in the final draft). We work so hard in our culture to build up our self-esteem that we struggle with this humility thing. The world has encouraged us to "look out for number one" and love ourselves first.

I saw a Facebook ad yesterday that said, "Have you ever loved someone so much you were willing to sacrifice everything for them? Well, love yourself like that and have the best life possible!" The marketers probably don't understand how selfish that statement is. Or maybe they do and don't care. Either way, they are wrong. Loving yourself first isn't the answer to a fulfilling life.

Loving God enough to let Him teach you how to love others and let Him love you is.

I always found it interesting the order of the Great Commandment as Jesus explains how love works.

Hear, O Israel: The Lord our God, the Lord is one. And you shall love the Lord your God with all your heart and with all your soul and with all your mind and with all your strength. The second is this: 'You shall love your neighbor as yourself.' There is no other commandment greater than these.

— Mark 12:29-31

Love God, love your neighbor, love yourself. Here's the cool part: where the Greeks had several words that meant 'love' in their language, the word here is the only one capable of describing divine love, unconditional love, love that transcends circumstances, personalities, environments, or bloodlines. And this root word, *agape*, is used every time in this passage.

Agapeseis God, *agapeseis* your neighbor, *agapaseis* yourself. The kind of love is not different. What changes us is the order. In fact, the order changes everything.

God is not asking us to love ourselves less. He's asking us to *think* of ourselves less. This is very similar to some teaching these days about humility. I've heard pastors say from the pulpit, "Humility isn't thinking less of yourself; it is thinking of yourself less."

Praying right now that this settles in your heart. We have to rethink (repent of) the part of us that is afraid we won't matter if we don't put ourselves first. You don't "take a backseat" to everything by thinking of yourself less. God honestly propels you forward as you learn to think of Him first, think of others next, and then think of yourself. You are not last in line. You are third among equals.

The model of this for me is the Trinity. God the Father, God the Son, God the Spirit—all always present, but each played a role. In the Old Testament, we see much of the Father in action, with the Son and the Spirit making cameos. In the Gospels, we see the Son in action, with the Father and the Spirit making cameos. In the letters, we see much of the Spirit, with the Son and the Father making strong appearances.

None of the three is less, but the order was used to change everything.

If the Spirit, who is God, can hover over the waters in creation, influence a few men and women in the course of history, validate the Son's mission, and wait patiently to be unleashed at Pentecost, how can I, in my frustration, rush boldly into the Church and the world with my own agenda?

No. I will wait, I will pray, and I will respond under the authority of my Father.

I will screw that up. Make a mess of it. Lose sleep and friends out of my frustration.

Then I will rethink (repent of) what I have done and come to the same conclusions.

Which will cause me to wait, pray, and respond under the authority of my Father.

From now until the Second Coming of the Christ, world without end. Amen.

PART 3

LIVE

THE HEART: My Kingdom or God's Kingdom?

I believe God is more interested in our eternity than He is in our temporary status. Yes, He is present and interested in what happens here on earth, but largely in the context of how it prepares us for a limitless future. This isn't an oversight of His. He has the benefit of eternal perspective.

Once saw Francis Chan put a piece of colored tape at the end of an extremely long rope to illustrate how our earthly lives compare to our time in eternity. It's a helpful way of envisioning it, but I'm sure he knows even this is a shallow understanding. We can see it this way, so I applaud his ingenuity. But it still doesn't capture the immensity of eternity.

Maybe this will explain what I mean. Think of your lifetime as the planet earth. Seems huge when we try to travel it, right? I recently moved from Indiana to Oklahoma, and let me tell you, it's a long way when you have dogs and kids and a big UHaul truck full of your belongings. I once flew to Bulgaria, and it took as long to fly in a jumbo jet to get there as it did to drive the UHaul from Indiana to Oklahoma. Vast. Immense.

Pull back. You are now looking at our solar system. Doesn't seem so big now, does it? Pull back some more and see our galaxy. How vast is earth again? Pull back and see the entire universe. Now, consider the universe is ever-expanding.

That's the difference between your life on earth and your eternity. It's not just a blip on a timeline; it's a speck that is minimalized in all directions by the vastness of space. Eternity isn't a really long time—it's outside of time.

When I contemplate how God works in us, I would expect Him to start with what is eternal in us because everlasting life is greater in every way than our lifetimes here. When I read the Great Commandment in Mark 12:29-31, I was surprised to find that Jesus quotes God the Father, and He starts with the heart.

I don't know how much stock we should put into this, but I don't think the order of words is unimportant. I've heard it is a part of the culture of Jewish writers to pay heed to how they express things this way. What is said first in Scripture has a different kind of weight.

For instance, in the Gospel of John, the 'disciple whom Jesus loved' talks about the difference between what Jesus brought to the world and what Moses brought to the Jewish people.

For the law was given through Moses; grace and truth came through Jesus Christ.

— John 1:17

Notice the comparison is not between the Law of Moses and the grace of Jesus. John is deliberate when he juxtaposes the Law with 'grace and truth.' Jesus said He didn't come to abolish the Law but to fulfill it, so grace wouldn't be able to stand on its own—truth has to be an equal partner.

But it matters that grace was mentioned first. That doesn't mean it is more important than truth; it just means that the grace offered by Christ tempers the truth that can still be found in the Law. We don't surrender the Law—no, grace *enhances* the Law, which is why the Sermon on the Mount is full of 'you have heard it said' followed by the Spirit of the commandment and not the letter of the commandment.

Grace is at the heart of the truth of God.

So, I would expect when Jesus tells us to love God that He would start with loving him with all our souls. But He starts with the heart instead. So, I did a little study on that and found out that "soul" in Mark 12:30 didn't mean what I thought it meant.

This will be fleshed out in the next section, but here's a quick primer. In his first letter to the Thessalonians, Paul is wrapping up when he writes:

Now may the God of peace Himself sanctify you com-pletely, and may your whole spirit and soul and body be kept blameless at the coming of our Lord Jesus Christ.
— 1 Thessalonians 5:23

A quick look at Strong's concordance shows us that "spirit" and "soul" are different Greek words. The first, *pneuma*, can mean spirit or breath or wind (some think it's all three at once, but that's not in Strong's). The translators typically call this spirit.

The second word is *psyche,* and it may be more familiar to us. It can also mean breath but more often means the seat of affections and will. This is why we call the scientific study of the mind and behavior *psychology*. In other words, the identity, the distinctive way of making decisions. It's not just how we think; it's how we respond to our world.

So, when Jesus tells us to love God, I believe He intentionally starts by telling us to love Him with all our hearts before telling us to love Him with all our souls. It's also why He spends so much time talking about the heart in His teaching and not so much on our soul.

He knows our hearts often drive our souls and our minds and our strength. How we are fashioned from the inside will dictate who we are and what we believe, how we think, and what we do. True, what we do and think and how we decide can affect our hearts, but if we want real change, we start in the heart.

THE HEART OF THE MATTER

I love that Scripture is not silent on the shortcomings of the Greats of the Faith. Not only does it make them feel more human, it helps me process my own issues with sin. There, I said it. Sin.

If that word offends you, maybe it would be good for you to hear that it offends me, too. The last thing I want people to think about when they look at me is the word sin. I commit them, and I struggle with that nature, and I'm sure everyone else does. But it offends me when people are willing to call my hangups and mistakes and errors and rebellion sin.

Know who else is offended? God. Not by the word but by my avoidance. The longer I take to confess what I am doing is sin, the harder for Him to save me from it. He wants us to have an everlasting relationship with Him, so He's not going to back down. Sin is what separates us from Him, so we have to live with the word.

Even when we are forced to apply it to ourselves.

David had a problem with that, too. Reading the account of what might be his greatest sinful episode (2 Kings 11), I can almost imagine him justifying himself. "It's not my fault she was bathing on the roof where I could see her. It's not *only* my fault she cheated on her husband. It's not my fault Uriah wouldn't sleep with his wife so that he could think the baby was his. It's not my fault he forced me to orchestrate his death."

Wow. What a list. But we are often lost in those conversations with ourselves. Our sins might be categorized as lesser against that list, but we do the same thing with them. "It's not my fault my wife stopped paying attention to me. It's not my fault the boss doesn't pay me enough, and I have to fudge my numbers. It's not my fault I had to lie to get what I wanted. It's not my fault they gave me too much change."

"It's not my fault that I respond to my frustration with wrath, sarcasm, complaining, and causing division...."

Hmm. Ouch.

When Nathan approached David and helped him to see his sin, one of David's responses was to write Psalm 51. Every time I read it, I'm amazed at the depth of his confession and the desire it breeds in him to return to a right and good relationship with his God.

Have mercy on me, O God, according to Your steadfast love; according to Your abundant mercy, blot out my transgressions. Wash me thoroughly from my iniquity, and cleanse me from my sin!

— Psalm 51:1-2

Though David calls on the love of God, the first two verses are dedicated to his confession. He realizes what he deserves and why. Over the course of decades, the kings of Israel and Judah are going to forget this more often than not: obedience brings blessing, and disobedience brings a curse.

David expresses his awareness of his need for mercy, knowing his sin has given God reason to curse him. It's an anguished cry that starts with a recognition of his position and then turns to what it has done to his relationship with God.

For I know my transgressions, and my sin is ever before me. Against You, You only, have I sinned and done what is evil in Your sight, so that You may be justified in Your words and blameless in Your judgment.
— Psalm 52:3-4

Rather than continue to justify, David rethinks (repents of) his actions and admits that his sin has given God no choice but to pass judgment on him. I sometimes wonder how often I really get to this place. I'm really good at telling God I'm sorry, but I don't always let myself really face the truth that my sin gives God this right. He would be justified if He chose to condemn me.

David goes on to admit that in his humanness, he is different than God. Where God delights in truth and wisdom, David has been led astray from both for the sake of momentary pleasure. At the end of this admission is a curious phrase.

…You teach me wisdom in the secret heart.
— Psalm 51:6b

Don't pass over that. David is not just being poetic here. He realizes the heart is where wisdom needs to reside. Not just a noun describing the process of making good decisions; wisdom comes from who we are as much as what we know and decide.

David doesn't mince words. *Purge me*, he says. *Wash me*, he continues. This isn't a comfortable process he's talking about. Yet he knows if God will but do these things for him, he will experience the restoration and, therefore, the joy he seeks. Once he gives God permission to cleanse him, he moves into a new collection of verbs.

Create in me a clean heart, O God, and renew a right spirit within me. Cast me not away from your presence and take not your Holy Spirit from me. Restore to me the joy of your salvation and uphold me with a willing spirit.

— Psalm 51:10-11

Create. Renew. Restore. Uphold.

Look where it starts. The Hebrew root for the word *create* in this passage is the same as in the very first verse of the Bible, "In the beginning, God created…." David is not asking for forgiveness. He wants God to make something completely new in him. Then God can renew a right spirit. Then He can restore the joy of salvation. Then David knows he will be upheld with a willing spirit.

The heart change is the root of David's prayer. He goes on to tell God how he will respond once his prayer is answered. As I read through the rest of that passage (I encourage you to stop and do the same now), I am struck by something.

Having sinned, David confesses and asks God to help him rethink (repent) and become someone new, someone wiser, someone who follows His will. He doesn't wallow in it, then. He prepares himself to help others to avoid the traps that have so easily ensnared him. He doesn't kneel and ask for forgiveness and believe he has received it, standing up and going, "Whew! That was a close one! I'll do better next time!"

No, he recognizes his own sin; confession, repentance, and renewal uniquely position him to help the "transgressors and sinners" in his sphere of influence. In case you've lost the process in my explanation, here it is, simplified:

1. Confess
2. Recognize my plight. (Repent 1)
3. Admit God is justified to condemn me. (Repent 2)
4. Ask Him to create in me the ability to rethink what is right and good. (Repent 3)
5. Believe that He is ready and willing to grant that to me. (Learn)
6. Share my new understanding with those around me. (Teach)

Better address that last one. I'm not suggesting David went around telling everyone what he did. No evidence of that in the Scripture. But is there any doubt the clean heart he received from God was wiser, more willing to see the temptations in life for what they are? He doesn't have to admit his adultery to notice the man who is considering adultery.

Sharing your new perspective doesn't mean sharing your sin. But it might.

I remember one year preaching to my congregation on Right to Life Sunday. We had collected money for the local crisis pregnancy center (apt but terrible name), and some representatives from that ministry were in the crowd. Preaching on something else entirely, I got to a point where I was supposed to share an illustration that helped people understand the person next to them might be hurting from something they can't share.

God whispered to me, "Tell them."

He doesn't talk to me often, and it's almost always just a few words, but I know every time what He means. I paused in frustration and tugged on my left ear (a habit), looked up toward the ceiling, and whispered, "Really?" He didn't change His mind. I chucked the illustration I had planned (don't even remember what it was) and confessed to my congregation that as a sixteen-year-old, I was the father of an aborted child. No one, not even my elders, knew about it except my wife.

When the gathering was over, I waited around for those who might need to pray or talk to me. Two different people, one man and one woman, came up to me after and thanked me for my confession. They too had an abortion in the past, but they were afraid to admit it in the church. Both felt free to let that secret go in their own way. To my knowledge, they never told anyone else about their experience. Hearing mine, however, helped them to heal.

I confessed the actual sin, and they didn't, yet all of us received some healing that day.

Your heart is sick with sins and secrets. Your frustration has sometimes brought the worst out in you, but it might not be the thing you need to deal with right now. Don't read another word, dear brother and sister, until you confess it to God.

Now that I have encouraged you to pour out your heart, please listen to the rest of this.

God wants you to experience sorrow for your sin, but He wants godly sorrow, not wallowing. Paul addresses this in his second letter to the Corinthians. He had to call out the believers there for some practices that were making a mockery of the faith. He wanted them to understand the danger they were in and be sorry for it. But not forever. If they were repentant—if they rethought their way of life and aligned themselves once again with God—they were free once more.

For even if I made you grieve with my letter, I do not regret it—though I did regret it, for I see that that letter grieved you, though only for a while. As it is, I rejoice, not because you were grieved, but because you were grieved into repenting. For you felt a godly grief, so that you suffered no loss through us.

— 2 Corinthians 7:8-9

Notice here the Corinthians realized they were wrong. It hurt them, made them sad, disappointed with themselves, and gave them a reason to fear. But only for a little while. Instead of staying in that worldly grief (I've done something wrong!

I'm a bad person!), they moved into godly grief and began to rethink (repent of) their sins. Because of this, Paul could continue.

For godly grief produces a repentance that leads to salvation without regret, whereas worldly grief produces death.
— *2 Corinthians 7:10*

The believers moved from apology and sorrow to change. God created in them a clean heart and renewed a right spirit in them. What could they do but rejoice that they had been not only forgiven, but changed?

Too often in my early years as a Christian, I would confess a sin, ask forgiveness, believe God granted that forgiveness but punish myself for my sin. I would wallow in it, cry about it, rail against it, keeping myself from spiritual things like prayer and church because I wasn't worthy. Think about that. No, *rethink* that. God chose to forgive me, to give me a clean heart, but I decided He would be more satisfied if I punished myself.

Who's in charge here?

Here is your first task to live out what you are becoming in light of the teaching. Confess and repent (rethink), then release the guilt and learn from it.

Fellow frustrated; you might not think right now you have sinned in your frustration. Maybe you haven't. I sure have. And I needed to write this down partly so I could remember it. I need Jesus still. I don't have it all together. I sometimes let my temper go when something happens that thwarts the mission of the church or makes me doubt my faith. When church members act unchristian, I make snide remarks. When denominations or megachurches suffer because another leader has fallen, I go into a frenzy. Blood in the water! Shark week!

Confess. Repent (rethink). Release. Learn. Teach.

If you're like me, this is going to take some time. God believes your heart—who you are; no, better, who you will be—is worth it. Don't just rush off to the next chapter if you haven't done this. You're going to need the kind of strength this brings to do the next thing.

THE SOUL: What Will We Decide?

By this we shall know that we are of the truth and reassure our heart before Him: for whenever our heart condemns us, God is greater than our heart and He knows everything.

— 1 John 3:19-20

Mack Slocum was a businessman who went to the same Sunday School class my girlfriend's parents attended. He always wore a suit and tie on Sunday. I always wore dirty, holey jeans and whatever half-clean, half-decent shirt I could find. We were like that old TV show "The Odd Couple" in real life. He was Felix, the neat freak, and I was Oscar, the slob, but he took an interest in me.

When he saw I was seriously trying to understand who Jesus was (that's how I would have phrased it then), he challenged me to go on a journey with him through the book of 1 John. He asked me to read chapters one and two on Monday, two and three on Tuesday, three and four on Wednesday, four and five on Thursday, and the whole book on Friday. On Sunday, he would ask me what I had learned.

I read that first letter from John for about three months. By the end of it, I knew who Jesus *is* and was ready to give my life to him. Those five short chapters are important to me, so I'm excited to use them here. And hey, Mack, if you're reading this: Thank you.

Listen to John's wisdom.

He just told us in 1 John 3:11-15 that the message from the beginning is to love one another with humility. Using Cain (the man in Genesis who killed his brother out of jealousy) as a reference, he tells us not to try to tear others down (murder them, so to speak) who are more righteous than us. Then he says in 1 John 3:16-18 that we should do the opposite of Cain. We should lay down our lives for them. Then he writes the verse above.

Laying down our lives and choosing not to tear down those whom God blesses is how we know we are of the truth. By this and by the next truth he is about to share, our hearts can be reassured. What is that second piece of wisdom? That when our hearts condemn us, God is greater than our hearts and He knows everything.

When I was learning who Jesus is, this verse meant God was willing to forgive anything. Now that I'm more mature, I realize this verse means God is willing to forgive anything *in me*. Subtle but life-changing. My heart tends to get me in trouble. I want to be the pure man God intends me to be, and in Jesus, I already have access to that opportunity. Also, in

Jesus, I am not yet what He is calling me to be. I first heard this idea from Gordon Fee and Dallas Willard when they taught at a conference in Chicago. When I had wrestled the concept of "already but not yet" to the ground, it taught the same thing this verse teaches.

God is greater than my heart, and He is the one purifying me. I am not getting better at Christianity. I am being transformed. Something is happening to my heart that will help my soul.

THE SPIRIT AND THE SOUL

A great representation of this is found once in the Old Testament and once in the New Testament. The separation of "soul and spirit" in these verses can teach us a little about how we can learn to live through our soul and what we've been learning about repentance.

> *My soul yearns for you in the night; my spirit within me earnestly seeks you. For when your judgments are in the earth, the inhabitants of the world learn righteousness.*
> *— Isaiah 26:9*

When I stumbled upon this in English, I just supposed that the two words were synonymous, that Isaiah was writing as a poet and not a theologian. Truth is, maybe he was. But when I studied the words in Hebrew, I realized he may have pointed to a theological concept as well.

The Word "soul" in that passage translates as *nephesh*. In Strong's Concordance, this Hebrew word has several meanings: a soul, living being, life, self, person, desire, passion, appetite, and emotion. In other words, the identity of the person and the outflow from it becomes personality. If the next word was meant to be a poetic synonym, it doesn't mesh well.

The word "spirit" translates the Hebrew word *ruach*. This word in the same reference has listed as its meaning: breath, wind, spirit. Interestingly, the Holy Spirit is only called *Ruach Hakkodesh* and never called *Nephesh Hakkodesh*, which got me thinking about the passage from Isaiah differently. Try this interpretation on for size based on the meaning of the words:

My identity, my very personality, and all that comes from it yearns for you in the night; my breath, what makes me alive, the wind that blows through me and from me, earnestly seeks you from within me.

> *— Isaiah 26:9, Rogers' paraphrase.*

Eat your heart out, Eugene Peterson. In the New Testament, Paul has an interesting verse in his first letter to the Thessalonians, the one we mentioned earlier.

Now may the God of peace himself sanctify you completely, and may your whole spirit and soul and body be kept blameless at the coming of our Lord Jesus Christ.

> *— 1 Thessalonians 5:23*

The God of peace (this means wholeness, not absence of conflict) is being called upon to make us completely holy (sanctify us) the way God intended. Then Paul adds a prayer that every part of us, the entire whole, would be kept blameless. Our soul, our spirit, and our body.

Here, soul is the Greek word *psyche*. Strong's says it can mean the vital breath of life or the seat of affections and will; the self, a human person, an individual. Though it can be used for breath, it is not used for wind or spirit. The thrust of its definition has to do with our identity, who we are as individuals. As I said before, that's why we call the science of the mind, as it affects behavior in all its contexts *psychology*.

The Greek word used for spirit is *pneuma*. Again, this word means wind, breath, spirit. In Greek, the Scriptures always call The Holy Spirit *Pneuma Hagion* and never call Him *Psyche Hagion*.

What I get from this is that our *ruach*, our *pneuma*, is somehow best understood when we consider the Holy Spirit working in our lives. We aren't all a part of God—this takes the teaching too far—but this may have a connection to mankind being made in the image of God. Something godly is already in us that earnestly seeks our Creator. A divine spark, if you will. What we have in us that seeks God can be separated sometimes from who we are and how we see the world.

That would be our *nephesh*, our *psyche*. The perspective we have, the way we handle things, our personality, and our identity. When it comes time to make decisions, those choices will be based on how we see life. If we see life (*nephesh*) through

God's image (*ruach*) we will respond differently. If our personality (*psyche*) is guided by God's perspective (*pneuma*), we will react differently.

So, when we talk about loving God with all our soul, we are really talking about both. For those of you who don't believe in the separation of soul and spirit, come back to us. You can believe this is two sides to the same coin, or this is two different coins—the result is the same.

God's perspective, His will, has been given to us so that we may use it as a lens for our perspective and our will. The Holy Spirit speaks through our spirit to our soul, and we become transformed.

THOSE ARE BIG WORDS. WHAT NOW?

What does this have to do with the frustration we've been confessing and the rethinking (repentance) I've been promoting? I'm glad you asked.

Whether we have grown up in a Christian family like my wife or outside of any Christian influence like myself, all of us have discovered how wrong we can be. I didn't need God to point out that sometimes I acted poorly and treated others badly. Sometimes, I could excuse myself because I didn't have the right information. Someone lied to me, or only told me half the story, or misunderstood someone else and then gave me bad intel on a situation. I acted on it and got in trouble.

Even when that happened, however, if I'm honest, half my trouble came from my response. Even if someone treats me badly first, I usually have an opportunity or can take the opportunity to decide to rise above how I was treated and meet intended or unintended harm with grace. But I didn't. From my perspective, the wrong done to me deserves a wrong done in return. Doesn't the Bible even teach "An eye for an eye…"?

Well, it once did. But now, a new teaching has come that reveals the Spirit of God, the grace of God, and the true intention of God. When we want to see things His way, we go to what Jesus taught because Jesus is God. So, what does He say?

But I say to you, do not resist the one who is evil. But if anyone slaps you on the right cheek, turn to him the other also. And if anyone would sue you and take your tunic, let him have your cloak as well.

— Matthew 5:39-40

The intention here is not to create a generation of sops who never stand up for themselves. Instead, Jesus is telling us to see things from His perspective. What matters more, that person's salvation or your justice?

I can tell you this is not my normal way of thinking. To do what Jesus is asking, I need the perspective of Jesus. To respond and react differently, I can't just rely on who I am and how I would respond or react. I need to see things as the image of God, from His perspective to even attempt it.

This is what Jesus means in the Garden of Gethsemane when He says to God the Father, "Thy will be done." This is what Jesus means when He tells us to pray, "Our father in heaven, hallowed be Your name. Your kingdom come. Your will be done on earth as it is in heaven."

God gets a bad rap for the times He disciplines His children. The Jews won't go into the Promised Land, so they wander forty years. The army of Israel conquers Jericho and then loses to little Ai. The Kingdoms of Israel and Judah go into exile.

Read those stories for me and watch how long God is patiently waiting for a change, how often He turns the other cheek when the righteous judges turn from Him and worship idols. If the Old Testament teaches us anything about God, the biggest lessons are His longsuffering and His everlasting love. We love to harp on the bad stuff (our perspective) without giving God the grace to see how He took the disrespect a lot longer than we would have (His perspective).

Why can't we be the same? What if we handled rudeness and disrespect that way? What if we, like Jesus, took a time out before jumping on the moneychangers and clearing the Temple? If we're going to act like Jesus, we need the *psyche* of Jesus.

We need His perspective to respond and react appropriately.

SO, ABOUT THAT FRUSTRATION

The lesson here is that we need God's perspective connected to our hearts so that our response to our frustrations is His response. Though the Holy Spirit is the same for all of us, each of us has a unique identity, personality, and *psyche* from which we respond. The only thing that perfects our reaction to the things that frustrate us is to rethink (repent) situations from God's perspective.

If I am frustrated with my faith or my salvation, what is the root of that? Seeing myself from my perspective and not from God's.

If I am frustrated with the church and members of the church, what is the root of that? Seeing them from my perspective for God instead of seeing them from God's perspective for us.

If I am frustrated with the world and the opposition to the Good News, what is the root of that? Seeing it from my ability to change it and not from God's ability to change it.

So how do we rethink (repent of) our perspective and find a new perspective? This is why pastors, Sunday School teachers, small group leaders, and others in the church tell us to practice the spiritual disciplines: prayer, fasting, reading, studying, silence, solitude, journaling, and many others. The idea isn't to check off a list to prove you are Christian. It's to recognize and reflect God's perspective, God's response, God's reaction to these things.

Rethink (repent). Why do you pray? Is it to tell God what you want or to ask God what He wants? Nothing wrong with the first question, but your prayer life will change when you start asking the second.

Rethink (repent). Why do you read the Bible? Is it because you were told you should or because you can brag about it?

Or because you believe it is the best way to understand God's perspective?

Rethink (repent). What is the purpose of fasting? It isn't to lose weight or to appear pious. We fast so that every time we feel the loss of what we are fasting, we think about God and His perspective.

Rethink (repent). Why do we have to turn off all the noise and just spend some time listening to God? Because He speaks in a still, small voice to those willing to listen. ("He who has ears, let Him hear.")

Rethink (repent). Why do we journal about our prayer requests and our lessons from and about God? No one is going to pick them up later and publish them to tell others how holy we were. But we have written records of the changes God is making in us so that when we lose heart, we remember we are not who we were or who He is making us to be.

To love your God with all your soul, you need to know what He thinks. Fortunately, God tells us through Paul that it is our birthright as adopted children of God.

For who has understood the mind of the Lord so as to instruct him? But we have the mind of Christ.
— 1 Corinthians 2:16

Remember what we said at the end of the last chapter? The heart will make the soul work easier, and the soul prepares us for the next step. Don't stop now.

Father, I pray that Your heart has begun to infect our hearts with Your grace and Your truth. From deep inside us, Lord, change us so that we are prepared to see things from Your perspective. Speak to us as we pray, read, fast, wait, journal, and do whatever else You call us to do to understand how You see the people around us; how You see us. Then, Father, give us the courage to act on Your behalf. In the Name of Jesus and for His Kingdom and His glory, amen.

THE MIND: Rethink Our Thinking

The first time I found out where the Great Commandment was in the Old Testament, I was confused. Jesus is God—I believe this wholeheartedly—and that means I expect Him to be perfect. If He is perfect and He is God, then He should know the Scripture; but when He shares with us the greatest commandment from the Law, He gets it wrong. Doesn't He?

Hear O Israel: The Lord our God; the Lord is one. You shall love the Lord your God with all your heart and with all your soul and with all your might.

— Deuteronomy 6:4-5

Do you see it? Heart, soul, and might are mentioned. Mind is not! Yet we've already read what Jesus reported as the Great Commandment, and mind was definitely there. Why is it different?

Think of it as Jesus helping the Greek world understand the Jewish thought. Where the Jews would use *nephesh* to represent both the personality and the thought process, the Greeks made a distinction. Our culture being more like the Greeks than the Jews; this is a helpful thing for us, as well.

The word "mind" in Mark 12:30 means to think things thoroughly. If the *psyche* is our personality, our identity, our selves, then the mind is how we process things from that core. The heart humbled leads to the soul's perspective. The soul's perspective can then guide our way of thinking.

I need that. You see, left to myself, my thinking goes wonky. Let me count the ways.

WHEN MY HEART IS SICK

The heart has many issues, but pride is likely the most common, the greatest threat, and the strongest danger to us. When I am not humbled by the knowledge of God, I act as if the entire universe is centered on me. Hey, I'm just being honest.

Most of the time, I'm the starring role, and everyone around me is supporting cast. Sometimes, when they are especially important to me, they have a chance for an Oscar as best supporting actor/actress.

When I'm sick and my wife takes care of me, she is my trophy.

When my kids do something that makes me look good, they are my legacy.

When my friends are there for me in tragedy or, even better sometimes, when they let me be there for them, and I say just the right thing… Man, I love that.

When my boss gives me a promotion or my coworkers give me praise, it's what I deserve.

And the Academy Award goes to…

Well, me. I'm the one that made it all possible. Even when they are the best-supporting roles, it's only because I was there to support. I'm just that good.

Unless they aren't treating me right. When my wife nags me for the hundredth time to do the thing I promised to do? Hate that. I wish she would appreciate all the other things I've been doing.

When my kids (act like my wife and) do something wrong, it always makes me look bad.

When my friends infringe on my time with their problems when they know my problems are worse (and then don't even mention what I'm going through!), I tend to get annoyed.

When I'm underappreciated at work, everyone knows. Why shouldn't they? All my fellow employees know how invaluable I am.

I wish I was just being facetious. Too much truth in those statements for my liking. I heard someone once say we judge others by their actions and ourselves by our intentions. If I plan to stay honest, it's as true here as anywhere. I feel like I'm enough in touch with myself that I know I rarely mean to hurt someone. When a person is hurt by my actions, I tend to justify it with reasons why I acted the way I did.

This is what it actually means to give an apology. I share the reasoning behind what I have done or what I believed to be right so that the other person will understand. I'm right—or at least there's a good reason I was wrong—so if I just explain myself well, they should be willing to forgive me.

When someone hurts me, though, I don't want to hear an apology. I want them to ask me to forgive them for how wrong they were. Sure, they think they are right. Doesn't everyone? That doesn't change the fact that they hurt me.

This is how we naturally think when our hearts are sick with pride.

WHEN MY SOUL IS SICK.

I can't separate the two, really. My pride causes me to see the world from my perspective. Most of my time is spent wondering how everyone can help me attain my version of the good life. Seeing people as pawns sounds so heartless. Wish I didn't have to be that real about myself, but I can't write this and pretend.

My wife and I moved halfway across the country to plant a church where we knew no one. The group that helps us calls it a "parachute drop," like we are being sent behind enemy lines in the dead of night. No one realizes we were sent there to bless the community with the Gospel of Jesus. What a privilege to be called by God for something so important.

We got jobs in the community, started going to different hangouts. We slaved over all the important things—mission, vision, core values, disciple-making process, and everything an influential church does. People were going to love us! If we ever got them to join us.

Six months later, they still weren't joining us. Where once we saw people, we began to see potential attendees. How could we talk so they'd come? What should we avoid saying to keep from scaring them off? We'd have conversations and then compare notes.

Our intentions were pure. We wanted to help people share eternity with God. The Gospel was our motivation. But we treated them as pawns and forgot the one thing that would draw them to God the fastest. We forgot to love them.

When I see people from my perspective, it's hard not to think of the use they can be to me. When I see people from God's perspective, I realize how selfish that sounds, and I'm free to love them regardless of their response to me.

WE SAY IT OFTEN

Were I you, I'd be a little uncomfortable right now. We usually aren't this vulnerable in the church. Don't worry about me. I know that God has made me a better man than I am presenting here. I'm not trying to illustrate how evil all men are; I'm trying to illustrate how we naturally think. It's the way of the world when left to itself, which is why we quote this verse so often.

Do not be conformed to this world, but be transformed by the renewal of your mind…

— Romans 12:2a

But let's not get ahead of ourselves. This is an appeal made by Paul because of what he has been telling us for eleven chapters. In his letter to the Romans, he tells us all men have no excuse for ignoring God (1), especially the Jews who do it anyway (2). Fortunately, we need only rely on the righteousness of Jesus (3) and put Abraham's kind of faith in Him to be saved (4).

We are whole through God's goodness, as original grace trumps original sin (5). So, we should pledge allegiance to Jesus and obey Him as He makes us righteous (6)! Once, when only the Law could save us, we were doomed (7), but we can now walk in the life of the Spirit instead (8).

God chose Israel to bring Christ to the Gentiles (9), but that doesn't mean He has forgotten the Jews (10). It isn't really a mystery, is it? God loves all His children, even if He must wait to save one child so He can reach another (11). At the end of it, he gets excited and produces one of my favorite doxologies.

Oh, the depth of the riches and wisdom and knowledge of God! How unsearchable are His judgments, and how inscrutable are His ways! 'For who has known the mind of the Lord, or who has been His counselor?' or "who has given a gift to Him that He might be repaid?' For from

> *Him and through Him and to Him are all things. To Him be glory forever. Amen.*
>
> — *Romans 11:33-36*

If you're like me, you just skipped reading that big splotch of Scripture. Please, please take the time to read it again. It's a celebration for the One who leaves no one behind. The passage means so much to me, I adopted the last verse as my closing for all my emails and letters. "From Him, Through Him, To Him" sums up what I understand faith to mean.

Paul leaps off that poem of praise to appeal to his brothers and sisters in Christ. Don't they understand how great are the mercies of God? He is worthy of our praise! No matter the sacrifice, no matter our brokenness, no matter the cost, we should be willing to serve Him with our lives. This is the context that introduces what we say more often than we mean.

God is too much for us to come to Him half-hearted, half-souled. Do we think we can come to Him half-minded?

Do not be conformed to this world...

When we think of pride, we typically think of arrogance and selfishness. My next confession is that much of my treatment of people as pawns are steeped in pride but founded in fear. I'm afraid I won't get what I need. I'm worried things won't work out right. I'm anxious about my lack of control over the situation.

We aren't just selfish. We're scared. When we are disconnected from God, we have no guarantee that things are going to work out okay. When we are disconnected from God, we feel the same. Unsure of the future, we manage the people and things around us as we try to bring about our desired result.

But be transformed by the renewal of your mind…

In other words, let God change your thinking to match His. Yeah. Rethink.

REPENTANT THOUGHTS

By now, I hope you see the thread God has shown me.

If my heart is humbled and my soul sees from His perspective, I will think differently about Him and about the people in my life. My wife won't be my caretaker or my servant. She will be my partner and my equal. My kids won't be my legacy. They will be my responsibility. My friends won't be there to serve my hopes and dreams. Acting on their behalf will be my privilege.

I'm not talking about giving up my hopes and dreams. I'm talking about God, so changing my mind so that my hopes and dreams will align with His. That's why Paul doesn't stop his sentence with renewing our minds and why we have to put the little *a* behind Romans 12:2 above. He goes on to make his true point.

Do not be conformed to this world, but be transformed by the renewal of your mind, that by testing, you may discern what is the will of God, what is good and acceptable and perfect.

— Romans 12:2

Honestly, I've quoted this verse too often without telling the whole thing. When I do that, I can easily think Paul is giving me the secret to bringing about my will for things. If I quote the whole thing, I can't help but see it more clearly. The point of thinking differently is not to get what we want out of God, but for God to get what He wants out of us.

I admitted from the beginning this was partly a selfish exercise. I need to repent of (rethink) what it means to follow God when I am doing it only for me. God doesn't want me to give up my dreams and desires. He wants to shape my dreams and desires. This is not a power-hungry deity trying to control my life. God is a loving Father who sees better than I do what's best for me.

Best part is I can trust Him with my hopes and dreams. He will probably change them, but only for my good. If I humble myself and look at things from His perspective, understanding His presence in my life will get easier and easier. As it does, I'll be able to discern what He is teaching me and where He is leading me. Whatever comes, I can guarantee this:

It will be holy. It will be good. It will be pleasing. In fact, it will be perfect.

91

STRENGTH: What We Can Do About It

By now, I hope you've figured out we can't do this on our own. In a later volume, we will talk more about the work of the Holy Spirit. For now, let's just agree that the change necessary to get our hearts, souls, and minds to accept this new paradigm is not natural.

We need something supernatural to help us.

The spiritual disciplines help us seek that help. We lightly covered them earlier, but only to make the case that they are necessary and that we should rethink (repent) why we do them. I don't know about you, but I get lost in that a little. As we talk about how to use our resources—our strength—here is the best place to start.

When we've cleared that hurdle, we can talk about some simple, foundational things we can do to avoid letting frustration be our main motivation. I don't intend to give a full treatise on each of the disciplines I mentioned earlier. My hope is to give you practical things to think about in light of our goal and then delve into them more fully in later volumes.

Remember, frustration is not a sin, but responding out of frustration can be. Walk away, pray, and respond under God's authority. Here are ways we prepare ourselves for the Spirit to teach us how.

PRAY FOR PATIENCE

When you were a kid, did your parents ever get you to pray this way?

Now I lay me down to sleep
I pray the Lord my soul to keep.
If I should die before I wake,
I pray the Lord my soul to take.

My dad found a paperback copy of Hal Lindsey's book, *The Late Great Planet Earth* when I was around seven or eight years old. For the first time, we started going to church. I remember suddenly praying at mealtime (for years, I thought instead of saying "Amen" at the end, we were saying "Dig in!"). We also prayed at night and this was the prayer.

Creepy.

I'm sorry if I'm treading on some sweet memories for you but think about it as an eight-year-old. Wait. I might die before

I wake up? And—And I've got to ask Him to keep my soul? What happens when someone takes your soul? These are serious questions for a third-grader.

After those scary words, we were supposed to start blessing everyone. Was that because God might take their soul, too? If someone I knew was sick, you can bet they made the list. To my knowledge, no one I prayed for during that four or five-month period died. I guess my first experience with prayer was successful.

I never prayed this prayer with my kids because I wondered if I wasn't indirectly taught something false about prayer. Look at the little nursery rhyme again, and you'll see it. Prayer means thanking God for saving us from death and making a laundry list of the people we want Him to save. Interestingly, I don't remember ever praying for someone who needed to know Jesus. All the people on my list were people I already loved, and I still was asking for a blessing for them and not for them to know Jesus.

Prayer became that for me even after I became a Christian thirteen years later. Thanks for saving me (and forgive me for this or that), and please bless these people I love. If you're a believer frustrated with the faith right now, you probably already learned that prayer is so much more. If not, that's okay. The beauty of God's grace and truth is that we don't have to kick ourselves for our ignorance or our disobedience. We just rethink (repent of) how we've done it before and start fresh.

Rejoice always, pray without ceasing, and give thanks in all circumstances; for this is the will of God in Christ Jesus for you.

> — *1 Thessalonians 5:16-18*

At the end of this letter, Paul starts throwing out little sayings to help the church become what God intended her to be. Rejoice. Pray. Give thanks. They are couched in other admonitions—encourage, help, do good, and not evil. If you read the context before this verse, you'll see I left one out.

Be patient with them all. Who are we supposed to benefit from our patience? The idle, the fainthearted, and the weak. How will we do that? Rejoice. Pray. Give thanks. When should we do it? Always, unceasingly, in all circumstances. How can we do it? Well, let me share the whole passage with you.

And we urge you, brothers, admonish the idle, encourage the fainthearted, help the weak, be patient with them all. See that no one repays anyone evil for evil, but always seek to do good to one another and to everyone. Rejoice always, pray without ceasing, give thanks in all circumstances; for this is the will of God in Christ Jesus for you. Do not quench the Spirit…

> — *1 Thessalonians 5:14-20a*

These last instructions for the church are written in a consistent order that will help us with our frustrations. Paul is admitting that the church of the first century had a lot of the same issues as our church today. People who are not contributing to the mission. Others are afraid to take a stand. Still others who seem to waffle every time someone shows some strength.

Paul tells us to be patient with them all and to remember what our role is among those people. Admonish, encourage, and help them. In case we think the first one means we can be as mean as we want if we are frustrated, he tells us not to repay evil for evil but to do good to them anyway.

Ugh. I don't want to do that. I'd rather complain about them, respond with sarcasm, and lament the end of the church as she was intended. The responsibility Paul implies is not what I am seeking. I don't want to be the one that stands in the gap for those people. I'd rather start a whole new church with the kind of people that will rally to the mission with me.

Only here we are, reading a letter from a guy who was alive when Jesus rose again and His churches are already experiencing these things. Humans! What will we do with them?

Be patient with them all.

There's a lie we like to tell ourselves about God. It doesn't feel like a lie, but it is, and it's a reference from the movie *Evan Almighty* (not that it started there), not Scripture. The lie is, "Don't pray for patience, or God will create reasons for you to need it!"

We tell each other some version of this, and all the Christians chuckle, and the girl on the fringe says, "That is so true." And we buy it.

Don't buy it.

Reasons to need patience are going to come whether you pray for it or not. So, pray for God to give you a supernatural ability to "be patient with them all." Frustrated with someone? Pray for patience with them and then ask yourself: do they need admonishing, encouragement, or help?

Rejoice, my friends. We are awake and aware enough to see the church is not all God intended her to be. God didn't make us aware so we could be frustrated. He made us aware so we could be an instrument in His hands to heal her.

Pray without ceasing. We are never in the wrong place to pray, and it's never the wrong time. We can even pray silently while we are talking to the person(s) causing our frustration. No one else needs to know. God loves the person who frustrates us. Pray that He instills that kind of divine love in our hearts so we can see them as He sees them.

Give thanks in all circumstances. I know— it's tough feeling grateful when we are frustrated. Paul doesn't tell us to give thanks *for* all circumstances, but *in* all circumstances. At least be thankful God did not give you this task to do alone.

Don't wait until the next time someone frustrates you to pray about this. Jump in right now. Stop reading right now and pray for patience with those who frustrate you most—your pastor, your elders or deacons or board, your fellow church members, your family, whoever it is. Pray for patience and thank God for an opportunity to be His tool to influence them with encouragement and help and joy, and love.

But don't just pray beforehand. Even as they do the next thing that frustrates you, pray for patience with them. If it helps, remember this truth: at some point, someone is going to be frustrated with you!

And don't miss that last part. Paul didn't just tag that thought with "Don't quench the Holy Spirit." He's connecting something for us. When we are impatient; when we don't admonish but punish; when we don't encourage but complain; when we don't help but respond with sarcasm; how can the Holy Spirit come to our aid?

ARM YOURSELF WITH SCRIPTURE

I like to have the Bible on my side. Nothing is more invigorating than to quote the perfect Bible verse to zing someone who is frustrating me. I've done it with elders and fellow pastors, family, and congregants. For some reason, I've never been thanked for doing it.

Reading the Bible is not about proving we are right. Frustration is the emotion that most often leads me to find a verse that validates me. Sometimes, I even use it in the right context. Still, the fact that "The Bible says so" hasn't won me a lot of friends and very few arguments.

I call this reading into His Word.

God wants to read His Word into us.

That doesn't mean He wants us to seek out passages that help us change the other person's behavior, either. This is a little less selfish but a cousin to finding verses that prove you are right. We can't read the Bible to prove they are wrong.

I call this reading out of His Word.

God wants to read His Word into us.

What is the purpose of the Bible? Pointing to Jesus. Jesus is the main character. I am not, and my adversary is not. Jesus is. When I read to make a point (I am right! They are wrong!), I miss the point. What God wants most is for us to sit at the feet of Jesus, walk with Him through his experiences, camp out in the Old Testament with Him to see His coming, and prepare ourselves to fulfill the ministry of reconciliation as ambassadors of His grace and truth.

You know this next passage well.

All Scripture is breathed out by God and profitable for teaching, for reproof, for correction, and for training in righteousness.

— 2 Timothy 3:16

We just forget that this verse is preceded by an admonition for Timothy. Look it up if you don't believe me. Paul is asking Timothy to follow his example. He's giving this truth about the Bible so that Timothy can be changed, not so that Timothy can change others.

Rethink (repent!) how you are reading the Bible. This is especially tough for pastors and people who teach classes or lead small groups. We seem to be constantly studying to tell someone else how to follow God. How often do we read to learn how we should change?

Paul is telling Timothy, "Brother, do you remember? I modeled the things I wanted you to become, no matter what my circumstances. Anyone who does it is going to be tried and perhaps even punished for it. But it's worth it. Be the wise young man your upbringing and study have trained you to be. You can find it all in the Word because God breathed it out for you to be complete and ready to do what God calls you to do!" (2 Timothy 3:10-17, Rogers paraphrase.)

Our first intention when reading the Bible is to find out how God wants to shape us, not others. Praying to see His Will and reading to see His Will, I will most often find out the person who needs to change is me.

FASTING IS SO NEW TESTAMENT

We don't hear much about fasting nowadays. I'm telling you, we should be hearing it often. Fasting isn't about going without food. It's about finding a way to focus ourselves on God.

The first time I really fasted was for Lent one year. I decided for those forty days I would not drink a single cup of coffee. If you knew me then, you would understand what a sacrifice that was. Actually, it might be a good fast now.

Coffee woke me up in the morning. Coffee kept me awake after lunch. I didn't know it then, but coffee also calmed down my ADD mind, as mild stimulants can do for those of us with that cross to bear. Coffee often accompanied my late-night writing binges.

I. Love. Coffee.

I told my wife so she could be prepared for my grumpiness. We also told a friendly couple so they could pray for me.

Ash Wednesday came and I made it through. Thursday, Friday, Saturday, and some of my withdrawals were beginning to wane.

Before I finish this story, I want to help you understand how this is more than doing without. Each time I felt a desire for coffee, I prayed to God. At first, I prayed for cool things. By Friday, I prayed first for God to help me keep my word for forty days. On Saturday, I prayed for God to make the forty days go faster.

Sunday came, and I walked into the classroom where I taught at my church. I was running a little late, so most of the people were already in the room. Sitting in front of my teaching spot on the table was a twenty-ounce Styrofoam cup from one of the local coffeehouses. Inside? Hazelnut cappuccino is my absolute favorite.

What could I do? My friend was trying to bless me. Should I ignore his blessing? But I had given God my word. Should I break my promise? Got to be honest, I blanked. I didn't pray, didn't ask God to save me or give me the right words. I just stood there, staring at the coffee like it was a rattlesnake shaking its tail.

Remember that friendly couple? The wife leaned over and said, "Michael, I forgot to get myself coffee today. Would you mind giving me yours?" Not only did I oblige, but I thanked God for saving me from myself. I went the entire forty days without coffee and experienced a deeper prayer life from it. Here's what I learned about fasting from that experience:

1. **It doesn't have to be food**. But it does have to be something important that will cause you to think of God more often. I'll be honest; it's more effective if it's food. Something happens around the third day of fasting from food that brings you into a new experience with God. If you can't do food or you aren't sure you should or can, pick something that means something to you.

2. **The timing is important.** Using food here as an example. Don't decide to fast when you already have lunch dates planned. Don't try to do it through the holidays if you have family dinners planned. The goal is to enhance your relationship with God, and that's hard if you find yourself in a position to break your word to Him or the people on your schedule.

3. **Tell the people who matter in your life.** The person who bought my coffee didn't need to know, but I was glad my friend did. When I fast from food, I tell my wife, so she doesn't plan anything for me (Don't have to worry about dinner, I do the cooking!). Tell the people who need to know to help you make the most of your fast.

4. **Don't tell people who don't need to know, but don't lie.** In Matthew 6:16-18, Jesus warns us not to make a show of our fasting. Not everyone needs to know. At the same time, if you get caught in a situation where someone is offering what you are fasting, don't lie! But

also, don't trumpet your decision. (Re)Think of what God may be wanting to teach that person by your confession about fasting.

5. **Stick to it anyway.** In every fast I've done, a time comes when I no longer see the point. That's when it's most important to have something to remind you. One of my tricks is to have a verse from the Bible especially important to me or to what I'm asking God to teach me, which brings me to the last item.

6. **Ask God to teach you something.** I know He can do it if I don't ask Him. Sometimes, I ask Him to teach me about something, and He chooses to teach me something else. But more often than not, He grants my request.

See where I'm going with this? If I want Him to teach me how to be patient with all, fasting is a way to position myself to learn it. He won't invent opportunities to be patient—they are already there—but He will make me more aware of my impatience. Feels like the same thing, but it isn't. In my desire to be closer to Him and to learn patience, I then pick a verse that helps me remember why I am devoting a fast to Him. This is the one I use:

Know this, my beloved brothers: let every person be quick to hear, slow to speak, slow to anger; for the anger of man does not produce the righteousness of God.

— James 1:19-20

DISTRACTING LACK OF NOISE

When I realized my congregation needed some way to connect more closely with the Holy Spirit during our Sunday morning gatherings, I was stumped. We were already doing all the stuff. Fixed the transitions and the flow so that we built toward communion to launch the sermon. Created a worshipful praise experience that bounced between the reverence of the old hymns and the emotion of the new songs. Prayed a lot corporately.

What more could we do? A mentor couple gave me some tips on how they do it, and I even got to experience their service a couple of times. Problem wasn't what I learned—problem was my people were different. They were never going to get that excited about what the Spirit was doing. Ramping up the experience was never going to make a difference.

God whispered a different plan to me. Silence.

Yeah. Silence. Like, no background music, no warm pad, no soft strumming or keyboard. Just silence.

I explained to the congregation what we were going to try and gave them a week to digest it. The following Sunday, we did a worship song and the announcements like always. Following that, however, we did our first prayer of expectation. I asked everyone to be seated and to pray silently to God. Tell Him what they expected of Him that morning and what He could expect from them. My final instruction was for them to stand when they were ready to continue praising God in song.

It lasted a full 23 seconds or so, and it was painful. We went through the rest of the songs and some other stuff and communion, and it came time for the sermon. I let them know what passage our focus was and what page they could find it in the pew Bible and asked them to reflect on their own what it might mean.

Then I shut up. For three minutes. Of silence.

If they thought it was awkward for them, they should have been me. We were streaming live at the time, so I got to stand there in front of the camera for three minutes waiting. I didn't know what to do with my hands or my feet. We sweat it out together, and then I prayed and started preaching.

Two months later, the prayer of reflection lasted almost as long as the three-minute reflection. We had a leadership conference with our board a few months later. Someone suggested we cut the reflection time to two minutes, and there was a mutiny. The board overwhelmingly agreed to keep it at three minutes.

Silence is scary for us because no matter where we are or what we do, the world is full of sound. If it isn't, we fill it up. We can't stand it. Three minutes of silence—well, 23 seconds of silence—feels like an eternity.

I'm an introvert by nature and know many other pastors who are. We know how to act extroverted, but the truth is we are drained by crowds. I like to get away by myself, spend some time apart from people and recharge. Read a book. Go on a hike. But most of the time, I don't even do that in silence. My earbuds are in, even if the music is instrumental, to keep from distracting me.

Yeah. I'm saving myself from a distracting lack of noise.

Until I realized recently that silence is where God speaks the most; when we shut up and listen, we can actually hear Him. I don't mean necessarily an audible voice, but I do mean something happens in my spirit where His Spirit can communicate with me on a whole new level.

No wonder He showed Elijah the strong wind and the earthquake, and the fire first. When we think of God speaking, we tend to go for the fiery mountain speech or the flood or some other natural catastrophe. But God, at that moment, showed Elijah He was more subtle than that. The still, small voice is how He brought His prophet back into the game.

I need that. Maybe you do, too. Frustration is often borne of the hurry and bustle of things. All of it is going too fast, headed the wrong way, full of sound and fury, as the old Bard said. We get caught up in the pace of the world and wonder why we feel so irritated and why we have such a hard time hearing from the Spirit.

Settle down, pilgrim. Sometimes, to find God, you gotta hit your knees in silence instead of taking on the grand adventure. Sometimes the silence *is* the adventure.

Don't just try it once. You'll feel the same way my congregation did the first time. Don't do it for others to see; you'll feel the same way I felt the first time. Just be still and know that He is God.

Read that somewhere, can't take credit for it. (Psalm 46:10)

WRITE IT OUT, LET IT OUT

Of all the disciplines I've listed here, this is the one that gives me the most fits. I'm too scatterbrained and impulsive to be regularly writing down what's happening with me. Still, I find solace in the fact that I have kept a record in the last six months of the prayers I've offered. Why? Because I get to go back and find out what prayers God answered.

To date, I've felt strongly enough to write down 85 prayers. When I finish the first draft of this book shortly, He will have answered 51 of them. Over half of them! I know because when He answers, I always write "Amen!" beside the prayer.

Can I be honest? Thirteen of them I wouldn't have remembered praying, and two of them have written beside them, "Closed door—Amen!" Yeah! I'm counting those, too! What I prayed for God to do, He chose not to grant. In both cases, what happened instead was better for me, not worse.

Here's why journaling is important. It not only helps me remember what God has already done and praise Him for His deeds; it also helps me believe He will do it again!

Remember earlier when we were commanded to rejoice always? Joy is not a happy feeling. Joy is confidence that regardless of the situation, God will bring us through. Sometimes, it does make us feel happy. Sometimes, it shows us why we should be grateful. Sometimes, joy allows us to grieve and heal.

Journaling brings all this out so that we can remember as we go into a new storm that God has been faithful. If He was then, why wouldn't He be now? Even if I don't get back to that journal for a week or two, I just pick it back up when I'm reminded of it. We aren't preparing a document for posterity. We're just getting in touch with the God Who meets us in real life.

Because real life can be tough, we need proof God is tougher.

A PROMISE KEPT

Remember how I told you we'd talk about those spiritual disciplines and then share some practical steps to move from frustration as a motivation to God as the Motivator? Well, don't pass up what I've shared so far in hopes of "really doing something." Allowing God to heal our hearts, souls, and minds is doing something. Really.

The foundation we've laid helps us figure out what the more visible actions should be. Without a change of heart, a new perspective, and a better thought process, we are doomed to repeat our history. Once we've started working on the places our choices originate, the choices themselves become easy.

So, this part won't be as long as the others. I'm just going to put out a few suggestions to help you handle your frustration.

RETHINK YOUR INVOLVEMENT

For those who are especially frustrated, we are tempted to leave the church entirely. We can't trust her to truly represent Jesus, so we chastise her from afar and tell people we love Jesus but we are angry with the church.

I was so tempted after I was thrown out of the ministry by well-meaning people who protected the institution more than the ministry. They thought they were doing the right thing. I wanted to escape my calling, my participation, everything but my faith in God.

But that didn't mean I was suddenly no longer "part of the church." So, every time I railed at the church, I was railing at myself. Would my absence make the church stronger or weaker?

But God has so composed the body, giving greater honor to the part that lacked it, that there may be no division in the body, but that the members may have the same care for one another. If one member suffers, all suffer together; if one member is honored, all rejoice together.
— 1 Corinthians 12:24b-26

We know the answer, don't we? "But that's not really the church!" Doesn't excuse us from our part as a member of the body. If it's not the church, then those people need Jesus.

If those of us who are awake leave them, where will they find Him? I know God can. I also know He'd prefer to use His children to reach His children, just like He used the Jews to reach the Gentiles and then used the Gentiles to reach the Jews.

RETHINK YOUR POSITION

What role do you think you play in your local faith gathering? I was guilty of this long before my calling. I loved to tell people what the called, trained, and ordained preacher ought to do. Before I was a board member, I loved to tell people how long it took for them to make decisions and how dumb some of those decisions were.

Then God drew me into a position at the church that warranted a seat at the table. I found out how hard it was to come into a three-hour board meeting after a long day working and try to think straight about things I only partly understood. We'd talk about needing a roof, and I barely knew how to swing a hammer. We talked about the plans for VBS, and I knew nothing about children's ministry. We heard the preaching plan, and I had no idea how hard it was to do just one sermon.

Then He called me into ministry. Had me trained and ordained. No seminary course can prepare a preacher for how mean and spiteful the sheep can be. They bite, I tell you. Sometimes, I have to decide between biting sheep and having no way to win. Plan the sermons for a whole year, and someone will still think I preached that last sermon at them on purpose.

What is your position at the church? If it's not a leader...

We ask you, brothers, to respect those who labor among you and are over you in the Lord and admonish you and

to esteem them very highly in love because of their work.
Be at peace among yourselves.

— 1 Thessalonians 5:12-13

Notice it doesn't say to respect those who do it right. It doesn't say to esteem highly in frustration and sarcasm. It doesn't hinge that esteem on their correct work. The passage gives no qualification based on the job those who are over you are doing. Paul just says love them, esteem them, respect them because it's hard enough without your respect.

Don't skip that last sentence, either. One of the ways we can love and respect our leaders is to be at peace with the other sheep. Don't discount the value; after all, "Blessed are the peacemakers."

What is your position at the church? If it is in leadership…

…shepherd the flock of God that is among you, exercising oversight, not under compulsion but willingly, as God would have you; not for shameful gain, but eagerly; not domineering over those in your charge, but being examples to the flock.

— 1 Peter 5:2-3

Notice they aren't your flock; they are God's. Love them the way He loves them. Willingly. Eagerly. Be an example to them so that they know how to follow. One of my least favorite things Paul tells the Corinthian church is to be imitators of him as he imitates Christ (1 Corinthians 11:1). He takes so much responsibility in that statement. Do I really want that? If I don't, I shouldn't be leading in the church.

The most important thing we can do is be imitators of Christ as we lead. And how did he do that? By serving. "The servant is not above his Master."

RETHINK YOUR POWER

Maybe you're expecting me to say you don't really have any power. In a way, that's true. God is the power that gives us salvation and sanctification. More than that, though, God has placed resurrection power in our veins.

Power is simply the ability to influence the behavior of others. The world tells us power is wielded through coercion, manipulation, and command. God tells us power is in His Spirit, living water flowing out of us for others.

Oh, you have power. The power to kill another's enthusiasm or to build up their eagerness to follow Him. The power to steal another's joy or to rejoice with them. The power to show Jesus or show your... self.

Rethink (repent of) how you are using your frustration.

Sister, brother, the church needs you. I need you. None of us can do it alone, and all of us want to see the Kingdom of God flourish. We might be idle right now, fainthearted and weak, but we are waiting for someone to show us something better. Will you step up? Leader or not, will you take the challenge to imitate Christ so that we can imitate you?

FIVE WAYS TO MAKE YOUR CHURCH MORE EFFECTIVE!

Cheesy, right? We see stuff like this all the time. More now that we have YouTube and Facebook and blogs and stuff. The internet is full of it. I promised you some practical steps, though, so here they are.

1. **Humble yourself.** Admit to God that you don't have all the answers. Admit you don't even have all the information. Rethink (repent of) how you have acted in the past and ask Him to show you a better way.
2. **Pray for church leaders.** Even the stubborn ones. Be specific. Ask them questions so you can be that specific. What are they deciding? What is keeping them up at night? Write it in a journal. Amen it when God answers.
3. **Learn patience.** When wrong steps are taken by leaders and unchristian behavior comes from the congregation, don't react right away. Walk away. Pray. Respond under God's grace and truth. Be patient with the idlest, the weakest, the scaredy cats. Infuse them through God's Spirit with your energy, your strength, and your courage. And listen! Sometimes you need them to infuse you. It's healthy for you and for them to admit that.
4. **Get discipled.** Look around for the person who is already exhibiting the kind of character you know God

wants for you. Don't ask them to be your mentor. Just ask them to go out for coffee. Express your frustration. Ask how they would respond. Thank them for their advice, even if you don't like it. Pray to recognize God's wisdom in their words. Act on them.

5. **Disciple someone.** The church can't change in a day (see #3 above), but she will never change if no one is willing to pass on the mission. Who in your circle is feeling frustrated and needs someone to help them cope with it? Teaching, you know, is often a great way to learn.

The Next Thing

None of this is easy when we aren't sure why we feel the way we feel. I started writing this book because I didn't know just how deep my frustration went. Learning a new motivation to help the church recover her mission sent me out of a great ministry into the world of church planting.

Guess what? It's there, too.

I can't escape what I'm feeling by changing my geography or my approach to leading churches. Only by letting God change me can I make a difference. I'm working on that right now.

The next thing, though, is to use the insight Jesus gives me to bring more healing to His Bride. I can't do that on my own, especially if I don't understand God's calling on my life. Funny thing, a calling. Happens differently for everyone, but one thing is always the same: the purpose. For the last five years, I thought my purpose was to change the church by sharing my frustration.

Turns out my frustration is part of the problem. Maybe God allowed me to live there a while so I could understand frustrated people better. Maybe He was just waiting for me to be quiet long enough to whisper in my ear.

"Michael, your frustration is your issue, not theirs. Write about that."

So, this first volume is about God changing me (and maybe you?). The next thing is to discover the Good News and understand it so well we can't help but live under it. Once we've learned that, we can be agents of change for the local church we choose instead of running from those faith gatherings. The next volume will deal with that. I hope you join me and learn what I learned.

I once thought my purpose was to call out the sins of the Bride. I understand now my purpose is to call the Bride back to the Groom.

> *"I, Jesus, have sent my angel to testify to you about these things for the churches. I am the root and the descendant of David, the bright morning star." The Spirit and the Bride say, "Come." And let the one who is thirsty come; let the one who desires take the water of life without price.*
> *— Revelation 22:16-17*

Let's walk this road together, inviting all to understand what it means to be invited to the Kingdom. Come, let us reason together as Isaiah suggested and see if we can't wrestle with the calling on our lives. This is the hope available to you: the faith of the frustrated who learn to patiently invite everyone to the Kingdom as we lean on the power of the King.

You in?

For Rethinkers Only

We were building something extraordinary. Prayer was infused in our DNA: prayer team, prayer e-mails, and prayer throughout the service. The Word was preached faithfully and effectively regardless of who was in the pulpit. Small groups scattered throughout the week targeted men, women, couples, and everybody. The children's ministry and youth ministry were well-served and thriving. We were growing in the Spirit and growing in influence.

My dream as a Lead Pastor. I wanted what every church leader wanted: to pilot a significant body of believers to become the hub of the community, teaching people to be disciples and reaching people with the Gospel. We had challenges, sure; not every decision process was smooth, and not every facet of the church was where we wanted it to be. Still, leading that church was fulfilling all my dreams.

Then this pastor from Bulgaria friends me on Facebook. We get to know each other, pray for each other, and encourage each other in ministry. Finally, he asked me the fateful question.

HAVE YOU EVER THOUGHT OF COMING TO BULGARIA?

I sent back, simply, "Nope."

But I promised to pray about it. So, I did, half-heartedly. I mentioned it to a few people I trust, and every time, their response was, "So when are you going?" I would tell them I wasn't going, but it's strange that so many people think it's a good idea. I talked to my elders, and they said, "We'll help send you." They were all acting so crazy. I went to my wife last. She has been a bastion of good sense for me and keeps me from doing impulsive things that get me into trouble. Surprisingly, she believed God was in the asking.

That's the difference between dreams and calling. Dreams are things we drum up ourselves. We imagine an expected outcome and shoot for it. Dreams are good, and they have resulted in many wonderful things in this world. Dreams are who we see ourselves becoming.

But calling is when God is arousing you from comfort. He's placing something in your heart that couldn't get there by itself but somehow resonates with who you are. We might never dream of doing it. That's okay. Calling is who God sees us becoming.

He had to beat me over the head with it, but I realized God was calling me to Bulgaria.

Pastor Alexander Vulkanov made a simple request with God's calling behind it. He set me up to preach five times in four days in four separate cities around Pazardjik. I didn't know the language, would have to drive a car, and knew not a soul. My cousin David Sekanic went with me as my right-hand man, prayer partner, and fellow missionary. Pastor Alex would meet with us throughout the day, take us to see the sights, and we would go over what I was preaching that night so he could interpret more easily.

The first night, I preached for about eighteen minutes. That's less than half my normal preaching time, and remember, half that time was Alex interpreting. Maybe ten minutes of preaching because when I stood up and looked out over the crowded room, I wondered if I would have anything to say to these people that made sense. We were from two different worlds. Pastor Alex told me the next day that I could preach longer if I wanted.

The next night I preached twice as long. When I was done, he looked at me and said, "Is that all?" He coaxed me to open up, so I did. I told them about a time when I had been beaten up mentally and emotionally. How I had been accused of things I didn't do, and how my character had been called into question. I told them I realized God was sending me to Bulgaria to heal me as much as to help them.

I didn't know how many pastors were there or that they would call me to sit before them and pray over me. The whole congregation was wailing for my restoration in a language I couldn't understand, but with a heart I understood perfectly. Then they lined up to have me pray for them. The praying lasted as long as the service. When I was finished, I asked myself why that didn't happen more often.

God called me to Bulgaria to call me back into confidence, back to His presence. He set something in my heart that night. Other amazing things happened to me in that country that are precious memories. God moved in ways I didn't know He could. I made lifelong friends with the Vulkanovi family, and my relationship with David deepened. But that one night in Varvara changed everything.

Coming back was harder than going there.

Who am I that God would call me into salvation? Who am I that He would call me into the ministry? Who am I that He would call me to Bulgaria? Who am I that He would bless me to stand there in the Presence of His Spirit and be blessed?

I guess, in a way, the person who left for Bulgaria never returned. I had discovered the difference between dreams and calling and dared to utter the words that brought Isaiah such joy and such discomfort, such bitterness, and such peace: "Here am I, Lord. Send me."

My wife and I left a significant church to plant another significant church half a country away. Geography wasn't the issue, though. My heart was.

IS HE CALLING YOU, TOO?

I shared this story to explain this final section. God changed me to call me to change me again so that I could respond to His call to change others. Is He doing the same for you? Stop a minute and think about this.

You can see the damage to the church and the damage some churches are doing and not be called. A calling isn't a dream of a church that meets your needs. A calling is never about you. He uses the gifts inside you in a way that satisfies you, but it isn't about you. So don't keep reading if all you want to do is change your church to fit your own image.

This isn't me calling you to arms. If it is, let me get out of that chair right now. The throne is for Jesus. Here's what He said to the crowd when they wanted to follow for their own purposes:

> *And calling the crowd to Him with his disciples, he said to them, "If anyone would come after me, let him deny himself and take up his cross and follow me. For whoever would save his life will lose it, but whoever loses his life for My sake and the gospel's will save it.*
>
> — *Mark 8:34-35*

The Greek word for "life" here is *psyche*. We've seen it before, haven't we? Last time, it was translated as *soul* and referred to our identity, our will, and who we are. For some of us, our lives have been wrapped up in our frustration.

For the sake of Jesus and his Good News, are you willing to lay down your frustration as motivation and become a part of the solution? If you are, I want to help.

The following are suggestions and questions that get to the heart of disciple-making. We'll discuss them in more detail in a later volume, but right now, this is enough to get started. I've gone back through the material in this volume and listed these prompts based on the reading in each section.

I'm not trying to get you to buy more of these books. You can if you think it will help, but the important thing is that it reaches you, and God used it to call you to do something to enlarge God's Kingdom. It will require you to trade in your dream of the church that fits you for serving the Kingdom that God is establishing on earth.

I can picture three or four brothers and/or sisters getting together, reading a chapter, and working on the suggestions together. That might be helpful, but notice this first volume is really about our personal growth, not our corporate growth. The choice is yours to do this with others or work through it on your own for now.

In later volumes, we will talk about real, encouraging, joy-filled accountability that comes from including others in our process. For now, though, it might be a solo journey. But don't let it stay a solo journey. Following Christ is very personal, but it was meant to be lived in community.

Become a disciple-maker, my frustrated friend. Use these prompts as you will; make your own when God prompts you. He is the one with the Power and the Presence, not me.

INTRODUCTION

1. How has the pandemic affected your faith in God? In the church? In yourself?
2. What are you relying on to grow your faith? Social media? Podcasts? Personal reading? Livestreams? How is this different from your sources pre-pandemic?
3. Are you fond of your current level of participation? Or do you feel a nudge to do more?
4. This one hurts. Are the actions of certain people in your past making it difficult for you to engage with the Church? If not, is anything else holding you back? If so…
5. When Jesus said, "Father forgive them, for they know not what they do, (Luke 23:34)" who was He forgiving, and when was He forgiving them? Do you believe He has given you resurrection power to do the same?

KNOW – TENSION

1. Begin with time in prayer. Not five minutes, either. Ask God to speak into your heart to help you discover the answer to these questions. Don't move on to the next question until God has helped you answer the one you're on:

a. Which of the frustrations in this section are mine? Are there more than one? Am I frustrated by something not listed?

b. Am I frustrated for myself or for the Kingdom? For both? How can I separate my frustration for myself from my frustration for the Kingdom?

c. How can God relieve the frustration for myself by using me to relieve my frustration for the Kingdom?

d. Is God calling me to be a part of this solution?

2. Journal what came to you in those prayers. Write them or type them so that they are concrete.

3. When you are finished, ask God to show you who is mature enough to receive your thoughts. Your pastor? An elder or deacon, or church leader? A small group leader or friend or spouse?

4. Share your thoughts with that person. Discuss it with them and the possibility that you are called to respond. Ask them to join you in prayer about it.

KNOW – TEACHING

1. How do you tend to express your frustration? Passively (avoid the church, reject conversations about certain topics, ignore certain people, etc.) or aggressively (vocal tirades, finger-pointing, strongly worded

criticism, outright rejection of the church in general, etc.)?

2. Do you relate to Judas, seeing good reasons why the church, if not Jesus, should be called into question? Have you rehearsed those arguments? Have you devised solutions for the issues?

3. **WALK AWAY**. Take some time away from the quarrel. Give yourself time to be silent before God and let Him tell you why it bothers you so much.

4. **WAIT AND PRAY.** Tell God how you're feeling. It's okay. Job did it. David did it. Habakkuk's whole book is about him questioning God's motives and actions. Don't hold back; give it all to Him.

5. **RESPOND UNDER THE AUTHORITY OF GOD'S GRACE AND TRUTH.** How are you contributing to the problem? Be honest. (I had to admit I was making things worse before I could see my way to making things better.) How would God want you to respond?

6. **RETHINK.** Are you called to repent of something before you can start being part of the solution?

BE – BELIEVE

1. Who needs to hear you ask them for forgiveness? Your pastor? Your leaders? Your spouse? Your friends?

2. Ask God to show you three people who may be feeling the same way you are. Talk to them about what you're learning and see how they respond. Encourage them to consider walking this journey with you. If you feel it would help them, mention this book.

BE – BECOME

1. True faith requires allegiance, not just mental assent. In that journal, make an entry where you discuss the pros and cons of allying yourself with others to effect change in the church.
2. Pray over that list and ask God to show you the dangers that may lie ahead if you continue this course of action. Count the cost of being a disciple-maker.
3. Decide if you are called by God to partner with Him in this endeavor to bring healing to the church.

INTERMISSION? MORE LIKE INTERCESSION

Don't go any further until you've given allegiance to the cause of Christ, have repented of (rethought) your frustration as motivation, and are willing to love the Bride of Christ the way our Father does. If you can do these things, the next thing is to approach your church leaders and discuss with them ways they are currently trying to meet the challenges of ministry to-day. You may be surprised that they have already been thinking about it and just need help implementing a plan. This requires humility, friend. Know who God is and who you are, and don't confuse the two.

Of course, I have no power to keep you from moving on before taking these steps. They are merely suggestions that I hope carry the aroma of God's wisdom. I just want to smell like Him if I can. I am interceding with the Father for all of you as a fellow frustrated believer who needs the Spirit to groan for me to get the words right.

LIVE – HEART

1. Enter into your own prayer of expectation. Write in your journal what you expect from God and what He can expect from you.
2. Revisit your entry. Which expectations are for your kingdom, and which are for God's?
3. Pray for God to give you a heart for change: yours and the church.
4. Realize God loves you and the church more than you do. Rethink His part in this process, then rethink yours.

LIVE – SOUL

1. What are you doing to train yourself to see from God's perspective? What can you do differently?
2. Make a list of people you tend to see from an earthly perspective. How many are Not Yet believers? How many are Already believers? Here is a test: Who are you predisposed to hold a grudge against? Who are you predisposed to forgive?
3. Read Matthew 18:21-35 and look back at that list.
4. Are you ready for a new perspective? Go back to the first question in this section and answer it again. Any changes?

LIVE – MIND

1. Attending to your heart and soul has already started to change your mind. The rethinking process has begun! Take some time right now to list five ways you've grown in this process, and praise God for them! Celebrate! Go get pizza or something!
2. All of the pieces should be starting to come together, but you will still find moments when you fall back into your old habits. New frustrating things will happen, and you will still react how you once did before rethinking (repenting). Don't be discouraged. Confess it. Rethink it. Start fresh.

3. Believe that God is slowly transforming your mind. If you celebrate Him when He wins and repent to Him when you win, you will find Him winning more often.

4. Let Him win. He's bigger than you are.

5. Don't let the enemy convince you that shortfalls mean starting over. Don't punish yourself. Learn God's grace and truth, lean into it and live it out, and lament your errors briefly. Godly repentance doesn't just produce sorrow; it produces sorrow that leads to repentance (rethinking).

LIVE – STRENGTH

1. Rethink your involvement in a church body. How can you be a blessing every time you gather with others? Every time you pull up in the church parking lot, ask God to show you why you are meeting Him there.

2. Rethink your position. Don't try to dictate to your leaders. Don't try to dictate to your followers. Paul asks us to imitate him as he imitates Christ. How can you lead by serving? (It's in the Bible somewhere.)

3. Rethink your power. What kind of influence are you on those who are Already believers? What kind of influence are you on those who are Not Yet believers? I really have to work on this one. How can I expect Not Yets to try church or respect the church when I show so much disrespect?

4. Set aside one day a month, or a few hours at least. Fast, read, pray, listen. What is God showing you that you can teach someone else?

   You may notice that by the time you are finished with this list, you are already doing most of the five things I listed that can help your church today. The biggest task left unmentioned is to disciple someone. It may seem difficult, but all that means is putting yourself in a position with others to let God's light shine through you to them.

5. Ask God to show you at least one and no more than three people who are willing to join you in your allegiance. They need to understand four things before they say yes:

   a. They are being asked to walk away from their frustration as motivation, to rethink (repent of) how they respond to the church.
   b. They are being asked to wait and pray about being a part of this group of rethinkers.
   c. They are being asked to learn how to respond under God's authority in His grace and truth.
   d. They are being asked to find one to three people to pass on what they learn when they are done with this group.

I've heard of people who are doing this and actually create a covenant they sign, but that is up to you.

VOLUME TWO

I'm working hard on the second volume as I finish editing this one. In it, we will explore the Gospel and see if we have fully understood the Good News Jesus brought us. You might think this is a slam dunk for you, but I warn you that I thought I knew, too. Working with a group called The Bonhoeffer Project has taught me that I didn't know what I didn't know.

For now, study it on your own. Look at the places where the Gospel is mentioned in the New Testament and think about it from a new angle. Talk to your pastor about it. If you don't have a pastor, go get one. We all need someone who is directing us and pouring into us or at least walking alongside us on this journey.

If you've gathered a group, study the Gospel together. Not just an account of Jesus' life, but wherever the Gospel is mentioned. Sharpen each other through your disagreements and debates. Celebrate what God is doing in all of you as you do.

Let me finish this way: the work of Christ is finished, but our work has just begun. Too many people today don't know. Help me reach them.

Even if it gets a little frustrating.

Author Bio

Jesus-follower, husband, father of four, disciple-maker, and content creator Michael S. Rogers is a veteran church leader, a frustrated-but-faithful follower, and a believer in the power of transformation for individuals and for the church.

www.ingramcontent.com/pod-product-compliance
Lightning Source LLC
Chambersburg PA
CBHW070513200726
48293CB00007B/2509